Salon Talk 3

Kismet

Men-Tal

Library of Congress Control Number:
        2013930297

ISBN: 978-0-9883374-1-1

Cover Design: Maurice Ingram and Men-Tal

Published by G Publishing, LLC

Printed in the United States of America

SPECIAL THANKS TO Maurice Ingram for always doing a magnificent job with the cover graphic design. Jay Jones for the crispy photography; your work is excellent and very professional. Venus Davidson (Cognac), and Amber Gordon for modeling. Quichard Cunningham for the editing of Salon Talk 3. All of the book clubs that have shown me major love and supported my books and events. Blaq Ice (President of the Chicago Chapter of P. O. E. T.) and BlackMaria (President of the Detroit Chapter of P. O. E. T.) and all of my P. O. E. T. family nationally and internationally for the 2012 Author Award I received on 12/15/2012. To everyone who has purchased my previous books and those who have spread the word about the Salon Talk series; I love and appreciate you dearly; without you, there is no me.

Reason for My Choice of Dialect

One thing that is seriously important to me is that anyone who reads my novels and follows my work I want them to have a thorough as possible understanding of my literary expressions. I believe it allows the reader to fully embrace the true essence of the particular part of the story in which they are reading. I had someone tell me they really, really enjoy reading the Salon Talk series, but they felt that I was a bit vulgar with my sexual expression in my intimate chapters. In every way do I respect my readers however when I write I have to remain true to the story; if I write it any other way it will be unrealistic. Prime example when people are having sexual conversations no man says I need some vagina, or Baby, I want to lick your woman-hood; that shit sounds corny. Now what he will say is I need some pussy or I want to lick your pussy. No woman says Baby, I need you to give me some penis or, I'm about to suck the heck out of your man-hood; she'll say Baby I need you to fuck me or I'm about to suck the shit out of your dick. Again, I do honor my readers and how they feel, but respectively I have to stick to the true essence of the moment and provide the readers with an absolute pure story. Thank you for reading the Salon Talk series and trust me you are in for a treat. This is perhaps Cognac's deepest story yet. So, I'm going to keep it real with myself and shut the hell up and allow you to enjoy the story. Peace...

THE MOMENT OF REDEMPTION

February 20, 2012 Downtown Detroit Michigan, 3:10am a truck carefully pulled into a very dark alleyway just in between two buildings. The headlights were turned off as the truck quietly pulled to the side and parked. Her large black Panama Swinger Hat veiled her face, hiding her eyes as she looked around the parameter vigilantly. The building to the left was vacant with a large filthy garbage dumpster up against it. The building on the right had three businesses connected to each other, a beauty shop, a shoe store, and a bar. All the lights were out because the businesses were closed. She turned the engine off and then reached in her purse. With black gloves on she pulled out a black automatic pistol and a fully loaded clip. She looked at her watch, and it read 3:12am. She slid the clip in, cocked the pistol and got out the truck shutting the door behind her. She wore all black and blended perfectly with the dark night; black body suit and knee high riding boots providing the perfect comfort. Her perfectly fit waist length leather jacket was just right; not to tight and not too loose. She looked around and made sure the coast was clear and no one was watching. She walked forward and peeked around the back of the building to her right. The coast was clear; no one was in sight so she proceeded. Swiftly she stepped across the wet concrete and carefully walked towards the back door. She unzipped her tightly fit waist length leather coat. The streetlights were all out in the immediate area providing the perfect camouflage. The faint glare of moonlight barely spilled through the sides of the buildings hardly providing any clear visibility. A stack of very old wooden doors with chipped paint peeling off were leaning up against the back of the building. She heard a strange sound then it suddenly stopped... Could it be someone waiting in the shadows ready to put a bullet through her heart? She paused in her tracks and looked around ready and willing to commit a murder. She didn't see anything so she cautiously moved forward. SUDDENLY OUT OF NOWHERE SOMETHING CAME RUNNING OUT FROM BEHIND THE RAGGEDY DOORS!! SHE IMMEDIATELY AIMED HER GUN; READY TO BLAST... till she realized that it was just a cat

Men-Tal

running off with a small rat in its mouth. Her accelerated heartbeat thumped rapidly in her chest. She took a deep breath and calmed herself as she looked at her watch again; it read 3:14am. She knew the moment of redemption was so close that she could taste it on her tongue. Everything was pretty much quiet as a ghost town. You could hear the faint sound of traffic riding by over on Woodward Street, and a couple of wind chimes hanging from above. This is the place she was looking for; she was at the back entrance of Lake's Bar. She placed her gun in her coat pocket and pulled out her lock pick. *I haven't picked a fuckin lock since I was younger. I know I can still do it.* She looked around and kneeled down making sure no one was looking. As soon as she got ready to pick the lock she heard somebody talking on a cell phone while approaching the door. Shit!! Quietly she stepped back, placing the lock pick back in her pocket and grabbed her gun. QUICKLY SHE LOOKED AS THE DOOR UNLOCK!! *Don't get nervous, stay focus. Just blow this niggas head off and get the fuck on.* Her heartbeat thumped a little harder, and her breathing accelerated as her eyes dilated. She gripped the pistol with both hands tightly. With a face full of anger and hate she got her stance and planted her feet firmly. She heard the turning of the door knob!! THE DOOR OPENED AND!!!!.................

HAUNTED BY GUILT AND FEAR

February 21, 2012, Tuesday 7:37a.m., Essential Beauty Salon... Regina pulled up in front of the Salon and parked. She was very saddened but holding her composure, trying to be strong. She noticed that Benita and Peaches had gotten there before her. She was also surprised to see Cognac's car there. What the hell is going on with Cognac ass? She hasn't answered her phone, and she always answers the phone for me. She aint in her truck; I wonder if she's even in the Salon. But if she was in there why wouldn't she have the lights on, and why wouldn't she open the door for Benita and Peaches instead of just leaving them outside in the cold? She took a deep breath, exhaled, and then got out. Benita and Peaches got out of their cars and walked over to Regina.

"How are you holding up?" Benita asked as she hugged Regina.

"I'm fine. I'm just coping and accepting reality." Regina replied, barely smiling.

"Well, you know you can count on us for anything." Peaches said as she hugged Regina as well.

"And that's why I love y'all so much. I'm surprised Coney's here. She didn't open the door for y'all or did y'all just pull up?" Regina asked, looking at Benita.

"Nall, we've been here for about seven or eight minutes now. We knocked on the door, rung the doorbell and she didn't answer. Peaches called her phone and got the voicemail." Benita answered.

"That's strange, I called her last night and she didn't answer. This aint even like her. Her car is here but aint no lights on in the salon. I wonder if she's even here." Regina replied with a curious look on her face.

"She might not be. Let's go in and see." Peaches said.

Regina took her keys out of her purse and opened the door. She flipped the light switch on as they stepped in. There was no sign of Cognac anywhere. They looked around and everything was normal as always. Regina grabbed her cell phone out of her purse and called Cognac. It went straight her voicemail and she hung up. Regina started getting worried and dialed her one more time. She got the same results...voicemail. Lord please don't let anything be wrong with my cousin. I can't take no more tragedy and loses right now Lord. I can't. Please... make everything be right and let her be safe. Just let all of this make sense. I know I don't pray to you like I should but please answer this prayer for me...Amen. Peaches walked to the backroom to hang her coat up in her locker. She opened the door, and was surprised and confused with her mouth wide open. She told Regina and Benita to come back there. When they did Peaches just pointed at Cognac sleeping on the couch. Regina was confused but glad to see that she was safe. They walked over to her and Regina shook her to wake her up. SUDDENLY!! Cognac rose up with her pistol aimed and fear in her eyes! Regina immediately dove on the floor. Benita darted to the side and tripped over a chair in the process, knocking shit down. Peaches just held her hands out saying don't shoot.

"Girl, what the hell are you doing?!" Regina asked, breathing heavily.

Cognac just stood there with her gun pointed, and hand nervously trembling. She lowered the gun and tears started streaming down her face. Regina and Benita calmly got up off of the floor and they all looked at her.

"Coney, what's wrong? What happened?" Regina asked as she walked over to Cognac feeling nervous.

Cognac continued looking down and shook her head. Regina never saw Cognac this shaken up before. She knew that it was something seriously troubling her; something far deeper than their most recent loss. Benita and Peaches walked up to Cognac as well. A very eerie feeling had come over all of them.

"Coney, what's wrong? Talk to me; you're scaring me." Regina said as she calmly eased the gun out of Cognac's hand and carefully sat it down on the table next to the couch.

Cognac hugged Regina and then broke down crying harder on her shoulder. Regina hugged her tight and started crying herself. Peaches eyes watered; she hated to see Cognac like that.

"Coney, did somebody put their hands on you or hurt you?" Benita asked.

Cognac shook her head, no and sat down. She wiped her face and looked at them and then looked away. Barely talking with any clarity she uttered "I...I don't know where to start."

Men-Tal

"Just start at the beginning, boo. We're here for you." Benita assured.

"That's right." Regina concurred, wiping her eyes.

Cognac wiped her eyes and regained her composer. She took a deep breath and shook her head. She looked at them silently for a few seconds.

"Okay...first let me say that anything I'm about to tell you stays right here in the circle." Cognac impressed.

"Of course, I swear it remains between us as always." Regina replied.

"Okay...then let's start from the beginning." Cognac said.

ELATED

February 13, 2012. 9:37a.m. It was another beautiful morning at Essential Beauty Salon. Regina, Benita, and De'Juan were styling their clients. Regina was whipping her client, Stephanie's hair, giving her that sexy, jazzy look. Benita was doing her famous sew-in on her client, Nichole's hair, and De'Juan was putting these stupid long eyelashes on his client, Belinda. The eyelashes look like they will make her eyelids strong as hell. Hey, if that's what the client is paying for then make it happen. However, Cognac had just pulled up out front and parked. She got out feeling chipper and smiling like she just hit the daily three digit. She walked in and everyone could feel her contagious energy.

"Hey, wsup everybody?" Cognac asked as she walked in.

"I see somebody's feeling good." Regina said.

"Hey it's a beautiful day today." Cognac replied as she walked over and kissed Regina on the cheek.

Benita glanced outside and then replied "Somebody must've put it down on you last night, and got you feeling good because um...it's a real ugly ass day if you ask me. It's thirty-three degrees, which means it's cold as hell outside. I had to shovel all that damn snow off my porch and down the stairs. I shoveled the walkway, the sidewalk and part of the driveway before I said to hell with shoveling the rest of that mess and decided to back my car out over it. Hey, call me lazy but my back started hurting. That's supposed to be a man's job anyway. Other than that I've seen five cars broke down on the side of the road on my way here. And I didn't eat this morning!" Benita stressed very animated.

De'Juan looked at Benita with a crazy look on his face and said "Damn Benita, I hope that gloomy lil storm cloud you got over your head today will stay on your side of the room. Your day sound's more hopeless than that 2012 dooms day theory."

"Why don't you shut up before I come over there and straight Dub-Step, and Crip walk all ova your bunion feet and make your day feel like 2012?" Benita responded, being funny.

Everybody shook their heads and laughed at them picking on each other. It was all in the name of fun and love so it's all good. Cognac proceeded to the backroom and went to her locker. She hung up her coat and placed her purse in the locker as well. She received a text message and checked it as she locked her locker. She smiled as she read what Devin had sent her which read "I hope last night still got you feeling good this morning." She immediately replied "I'm on cloud nine right now, and can't wait to get off of work so I can get back to you." Cognac walked back up in the front of the salon to her station. She had a spray bottle of warm water and sprayed a little on her chair. She grabbed a couple of pieces of paper towel and wiped her seat down real good. Her exultant energy was very noticeable.

"Okay, talk to me. What's going on in your world right now that got you so upbeat?" Regina asked as she looked at Cognac with a smile and a hand on her hip.

Cognac looked over at Regina with clueless eyes and innocently asked "What?"

Men-Tal

"What you mean what? Your energy is very contagious, I'm loving it, I'm curious so do tell. We need some positivity around here." Regina said, smiling with an interested look on her face.

Cognac just bust out smiling, and now everyone wanted to know what was up. It was all eyes on Cognac like everyone was watching the presidential debate.

"You must've got your Valentine's Day gift early?" Benita asked, smiling.

"I guess you can say something like that, but...better. Here it is. Devin asked me what I wanted for Valentine's Day, and I told him something creative and different from the norm. I also asked him what he wanted and he basically said the same thing I said. Now I know Sweetest Day is supposed to be for the man and Valentine's Day is supposed to be for the woman. However I just wanted to do something for him as well. So we both decided that we would start last Saturday and do something to please each other the whole day all the way up to Valentine's Day. And I must say that it's been quite beautiful thus far." Cognac said.

"Oh hell nall, I don't want the watered down version. I want the Real Deal Holyfield so come with it." Regina retorted.

"Okay well, Saturday was my day to be pleased. He took me to breakfast at Sweet Lorraine's in Southfield and the food was delicious. Then he took me to get the best full body massage I have ever had in my life. It was so relaxing and then we went and did a little yoga. After that we went back to his place and you know...did our thang and then later that night he took me to a place called Oasis." Cognac said.

"Never heard of that. What's the Oasis?" Regina asked.

"It's a beautiful spa like I've never seen before. It's classy, it's sexy, I mean...the place is gorgeous. When you walk in the Asian themed room, it had a fireplace. And what made it so perfectly different was the fact that it was one of their outdoor spas and its winter time. You can just look up and see the sky; I loved it."

"Y'all wasn't freezing?" De'Juan glanced over and asked.

"Nall, it was very well temperature controlled. Of course when you first walk out there you feel a little chill, but that's only for a second. We tip-toed to the spa in our sandals and beach towels. And when we got in it felt like we were in paradise." Cognac passionately expressed as she briefly closed her eyes and smiled.

"That sounds so beautiful. I mean the perfect stress relieving day." Regina replied.

"Oh my Gaud, it was the perfect stress relieving day. Especially with all the stuff I've been through. All the tension I felt in my back and in my neck; my body was calling for it." Cognac said.

"Okay, so what did y'all do on his day?" Benita asked, smiling.

"Well when we first got up I laid comfortably on the bed. I gave him a top of the line hot oil body massage."

"Did the massage have a happy ending?!" Benita asked very animated.

Cognac laughed and replied "Yes Benita, it had a happy ending."

"My girl; keep talking!" Benita said as she continued doing her clients hair.

"So after his HAPPY...ENDING...Benita, we got up, showered, and got dressed. I had a gourmet chef come over and fix us brunch. He sat his cooking station up right in front of the dinning-room table where we were sitting at. He had all the spices laid out on the side for us to choose from. He made us the most tender and Delicious prime rib. Scrambled eggs with cheddar, Swiss, and American cheese. We had herbed potatoes with grilled peppers and onions. We had freshly squeezed orange juice and Moet mimosas."

"Damn girl, now that sounds good right about now." Nichole replied, sincerely.

"It was, and then we went to the Charles H. Wright African American museum; where all black folks need to go and learn more about themselves. We went to a nice bar, had a few drinks, shot some pool, and played some darts. Then we ended the night off with a mystery train ride. They had live entertainment, singers, and poets. They had some really good food, and we played a really fun mystery game."

"Okay, I see why you're all chipper now, and you deserve it." Regina replied.

"What does he have planned for you today?" De'Juan asked.

"I'm not sure, but he can practically do anything for me right now after these past couple of days. But tomorrow Ima make him the bomb breakfast, and Ima take him to the gun range."

"The gun range?" Benita asked with an incredulous look on her face.

"Yes, the gun range. And then later Ima throw a curve ball at him and take him to the strip club." Cognac answered with a devilish grin.

"The strip club?" De'Juan and Regina surprisingly asked at the same time.

"Oh, you trying to rock his damn world for real!" De'Juan replied.

"Now you had me all in all the way up to this point. I aint taking my man to no strip club, that's out the question." Regina said.

"What's wrong with taking your man to the strip club? It adds a little razzle dazzle to the relationship." Nichole said.

"Hey, I aint knocking nobody else, but me personally I'm not into naked women. Besides, I got all the razzle dazzle and excitement my man need right here." Regina stressed.

"Hey, to each his own. I feel you Regina and aint nothing wrong with how you feel. At the same time it does add a little freaky spice to the mix." Benita said.

"What, are you serious?" Regina asked.

"I tell you what, just try it once. I bet your man will have you walking in here bowlegged the next morning. Coney, you keep doing what you doing. You about to hit a homerun this time boo." Benita preached.

By that time a man had pulled and parked out front. He got out with a few novels he wrote in his hand. It was part one and two of his series. He was dressed nice and well shaven. He stepped inside and had cool aura about himself.

"Hello, how is everybody doing?" The guy asked.

"Just fine. How can we help you today?" Regina asked politely.

"Well my name is Kenneth and I'm a novelist. And I just wanted to show y'all my books if that's okay and see if anyone would like to purchase some." Kenneth answered.

"You got some of them good, spicy drama novels with all the shoot em up, backstabbing and sex in them?" Benita asked.

"All of that and then some." Kenneth answered, smirking.

"Give me all of them!" Benita said, being silly yet serious.

"Dang Benita, sound like you done found a good fix." De'Juan said.

"Hey, I love reading especially if it's good. I read through them in a couple of days and then I be fiending for more. Do you mind if I take a look at them?" Benita asked.

"Sure, no problem." Kenneth replied.

"Can I see one to?" Cognac asked.

"Absolutely." Kenneth answered, and handed both of them a couple novels.

Cognac and Benita admired the book covers and read the backs of both.

"Okay, there both hot. I'll take both of them!" Benita said.

"Yeah, me to." Cognac said as well.

"Dang, they sound that good? Let me see." Regina asked.

Cognac handed her the books and she read both of the back covers. She immediately decided she wanted both of them. The spirit was contagious because everyone in the salon bought a book or two. Kenneth was very appreciative with all the love they showed him. It feels good when your people show you love and support their own. Now that's wsup.

Open Fire

Men-Tal

OPEN FIRE

February 14, 2012, Valentines' Day. The scream of rapid gunfire blasted off like violent fury! With one eye tightly shut and the other eyeing the target she blasted the head and torso several times. Yeah, take that! A mean scowl tightened on her face as she concentrated blasting off several more rounds. Flames repeatedly burst from the end of the barrel as shell casings ejected onto the floor. Every trigger pull was fueled by past frustration and the built up hate. Fuck you muthafucka Cognac said as the last bullet went right between the eyes, and she watched the last shell case flip down to the floor and spin right beside her foot. Damn, it felt good to let off some tension as she sat the gun down on the ledge and took her protective glasses off.

"Oh you think you Billy The Kid, huh?"Devin stood behind her applauding her outstanding shooting, taking his earmuffs off.

"What, I can't hear you?" Cognac sort of yelled with her overhead gun range earmuffs on.

"I said, you think you're Billy The Kid, huh?" Devin said louder.

With a cocky swag and a slick smirk she replied "Something like that."

The target started drawing to her as she stood there looking at how she did. Once the target reached her she took it off, turned around and looked at Devin "Now that's how you hit a target!"

Devin walked up to her holding his target in his hand down by his side. His eyes where fixated on her delectable looking bulging breast as they peeked through the top of her blue jean jumpsuit. *Damn I want to bust a fucking nut right between them big ass titties!*

"Well, I definitely see what target I want to hit." Devin said with his eyes zeroed in on her cleavage.

Cognac looked at him with a little stank expression on her face and said "Um, getcha eyes off of my tits and pay attention to my lips." Cognac pointed at her lips.

Devin looked at her moist looking glossy ass lips and with a serious straight face he replied "You know what? You're absolutely right baby; your nice ass lips would be the first target I would rather aim for, and then the breast. I don't know why didn't I think of that before you did, duh."

Cognac gave him that oh for real look and said "Devin, stop playing and look at my damn target. That's gone be you if you keep being nasty." Cognac replied playfully as she held the target up to his face.

"That's some pretty good damn shooting Ms. Lady. I wouldn't want to be on your bad side, and on the other end of the barrel." Devin replied, admiring her accuracy.

"You ought to let Momma teach you a little something, something."

"I hear you talking baby, that is how you hit a target, but um...this is how you lay somebody ass the fuck down." Devin said as he held his target up with shots through the head and neck only.

"Whatever, you just lucked up and got me this time." Cognac replied with a smile.

"Yeah, I hear you sexy girl, but that was the same thing you said the other day when I spanked that ass in Mrs. Pac-Man at the arcade."

"Oh, don't be talking junk, you only won by a couple thousand, and that's only because you kept feeling on me while I was playing.

So technically if you hadn't cheated I would've won."

"I know, I know but how can I resist?" Devin said in a funny voice, starring at her hips.

"Look at you, mind always in the gutter. Are you ready to go yet, I'm hungry?"

"Yeah, me to. I need some Cognac to eat, I mean drink." Devin said with a slick nasty smirk on his face.

Cognac just shook her head and grabbed her coat and belongings and they checked out and left. As they walked to the car Devin hit the unlock button on the remote. He walked around to the passenger side and opened the door for her like a gentleman. Devin got in the car and they pulled off. They decided they were going to go to IHop, sit down and eat.

NICE TO MEET YOU

After while, Devin and Cognac drove up 8mile and decided that they wanted something to sip on. They pulled up in the 8mile and Evergreen liquor store parking lot. They parked just in front of the store entrance. Cognac asked Devin if he wanted anything in particular from out of there and he told her what he wanted. Cognac got out looking sexy as always and went inside. A few people were in there buying drinks, cigarettes and other things they needed. Hell, it's Valentine's Day. She walked to the cooler and grabbed a cranberry juice, a papaya juice, and a cherry cola. She walked up to the counter and sat her items down. She looked up and scanned the variety of liquors they had. The cashier had just finished serving another customer and looked at her.

"Hello, will that be all?" The cashier asked with a smile.

"No. Can I get a fifth of Ciroc Peach, and a fifth of Hennessey VSOP?" Cognac asked.

While the Cashier turned to get her stuff a lady by the name of Nook-Nook approached the counter. She was very attractive, fair skinned, long hair, glossy lips and a nice shape. She sat her things down on the counter and just happened to look over at Cognac. Slight curious look on her face, she thought she recognized her from somewhere.

"That's a nice hat you're wearing. It has that jazzy swinger style." Nook-Nook said.

"Thank you; I love these hats. I get them in all colors if I can find them." Cognac replied with a smile as she looked back at the cashier.

"Is your name Cognac?" Nook-Nook asked.

Cognac looked at her sort of sideways trying to figure were she knew her from. "Yeah that's me... Do I know you from somewhere?"

"No, I just remember you from somewhere; your face and name stands out. There kind of hard to forget. Maybe we're facebook friends or something." Nook-Nook answered, trying to put it together.

"Probably so." Cognac replied.

"But nall... I think I remember you from a picture or flyer or something my EX brought home and left around one day." Nook-Nook replied with an inquisitive look on her face and the cashier rung up Cognac's items.

"Really...an ex, huh? Wait hold on one second while I answer this call." Cognac said as she grabbed her phone an answered it.

It was Cognac's son's father, Eric Sr. calling. He was letting her know that he wanted to stop by and grab lil Eric some extra clothes. He also let her know that Eric also had a fever of 101. Cognac instantly went into over protective mode. She started asking all kind of questions like a typical loving mother would. Literally the conversation she and Nook-Nook was having had become obsolete. The store cashier put the drinks and chasers in a paper bag. He put the paper bag inside of a plastic bag and told her the total was $79.58. Cognac pulled out her credit card and handed it to the cashier. The cashier told her that he needed her I.D. Cognac pulled her I.D. out of her wallet and handed it to him. The cashier looked at it and swiped her credit card. He handed Cognac her receipt, credit card, and bags. Cognac was so focused on lil Eric that she didn't notice that she didn't get her I.D. back. She told Nook-Nook to take care as she grabbed her things and walked out. The cashier realized that she had left her

I. D. He tried to get her attention just as she walked out.

"I'll give it to her." Nook-Nook said, looking at the cashier.

The cashier said no at first and then asked "Is that your friend?"

"Yes, I wouldn't have said I would give it to her if I didn't know her." Nook-Nook replied.

"Okay, hurry and give it to her before she takes off." The cashier said as he handed her Cognac's I.D.

As Nook-Nook headed out the door she took a good look at the I.D. Hmmm I didn't realize how much we look alike; I see why he was fucking with you. She opened up the door and quickly got Cognac's attention.

"Hey, you um....oh never mind." Nook-Nook said, about to give Cognac her I.D and then sinisterly thought to keep the I.D instead.

Devin looked up and said "I think that lady is saying something to you.

Cognac looked up and rolled her window down.

"What you say?" Cognac asked.

"Oh nothing; it aint nothing." Nook-Nook replied and proceeded to her car.

"Oh...alright then...weird bitch." Cognac uttered as she looked at her strangely while rolling her window up.

"Why you call her weird?" Devin asked.

"She's just a weird ass braud; but oh well; let's go, baby."

Welcome To Paradise

WELCOME TO PARADISE

9:38p.m. Devin and Cognac pulled into the packed parking lot of Club Paradise. They both grabbed a handful of flyers that promoted Cognac's annual party that she throws every February 22; the Status Quo Party. Cognac stuck half of them in her purse as she and Devin got out and placed flyers on all of the cars just before they headed inside. Devin had never been to Club Paradise and figured it was just a bar. A few dudes stood out front of the club talking; one dude was dressed in a suit, and the other two in regular street gear. Their whole conversation changed as they noticed Cognac and Devin approaching. They lustfully commented to themselves about how sexy Cognac looked in her curve hugging jeans. GAUD DAMN, AINT NO WAY THIS BRAUD ASS AINT FAT AS FUCK WITH HIPS LIKE THAT!! One of the fellas uttered as Devin opened the door for Cognac. Devin felt like a G as he paid those dudes no mind as they gawked at Cognac's ass while they walked in. They tried to get another good ass look in as Devin walked on in. "Welcome to Club Paradise baby. I told you I had a surprise for you for Valentine's Day." Cognac said to Devin as a surprised look appeared on his face. He looked at Cognac and grinned; astonished yet impressed that she'd brought him there. The ambiance was dim as the neon lights reflected in their eyes. It was a circular type club with a wood grain bar just to your right as you walk in. Mirrors were all around from wall to wall allowing you to see yourself from all angles. Six, forty inch flat screen TV's were mounted on the wall all around showing videos or sports. The stage was dead in the center of everything with two poles that led up to a mirror paneled ceiling. The low, deep baseline from the music touched the lower chakra as he looked up at the sexy stripper leaping and clinging to the top of the pole, and locking her leg around it. She slowly spun around with her hair flailing in the air. Cognac and Devin calmly walked through to find a seat. Men and women looked and stared at them as they passed by. Dudes and females were captivated, thinking GAUD DAMN as they gawked at Cognac's ass. Some women were just flat out jealous and gave dirty looks. They either felt threatened that she would absorb all of the attention of the fellas in the club, or jealous because she was strapped much better than them. Cognac and Devin found an open table up against the wall and sat down. The waitress walked up in her body fitting shirt, black satin boy shorts, fishnet leggings, and black heels. She asked them if they wanted something to eat and drink. They ordered some drinks, an order of fried chicken wings and some onion rings. After ten minutes had gone by the waitress returned with their order. Cognac handed the waitress her credit card and started a tab. The DJ announced that Miss Eclectic was up next. The dancer finished her set and stepped down. A very, very attractive lady stepped up to the stage ready to go on. She stood five foot five and a half with legs that were nicely toned and an ass that was just right. Cognac wasn't the least bit intimidated by any of the women in there. She got the attention of one of the tightest dancers and asked her to give Devin a lap dance. The dancer introduced herself as Temptation, and took a good swallow of her drink. The DJ put on a track called H.A.M and Temptation sat on his lap and started grinding him. It was ten dollars a dance that night so Cognac put thirty dollars in her g-string strap. Cognac ordered another round of drinks for all of them. Devin was enjoying the whole moment like a G. He walked in with the baddest chick on his arm, got the baddest dancer in the strip club riding his dick, and food and drinks to set it off. Devin was definitely going to be fucking the shit out of Cognac when they got up out of there! Temptation looked over at Cognac and said "Thank you for the drink."

"You welcome." Cognac replied.

"I noticed you looking quite scrumptious when you walked in." Temptation said.

"Thank you."

"Would you like a dance? It would be on me since you showed me love with the drink." Temptation asked as she continued winding and riding Devin.

"I aint never had one myself, but I can't lie and say that I haven't thought about it. Maybe in a little while before we leave." Cognac replied as she leaned over looking at the next stripper who was about to go on stage and dance.

"For sho sweetie." Temptation replied.

Cognac reached in her purse and pulled out one of her business cards and handed it to Temptation.

"If you ever need a hairdresser I do hair over at Essential Beauty Salon." Cognac said.

"Oh for real?! My girl go to y'all over there, and her hair be laid." Temptation said.

"Oh yeah, what's her name?" Cognac asked.

"Chelsea." Temptation answered.

"Chelsea Jamison?" Cognac asked.

"Yup, that's her."

"Yeah, I've been doing her hair for the longest." Cognac replied.

"Well, I'm definitely coming to you to get my hair done."

The DJ introduced the next stripper coming to the stage, Miss Nympho. Cognac had an inquisitive look on her face and looked at Temptation.

"Hey, is that Candace that's stepping up on that stage?" Cognac asked.

"Yeah, but around here we call her Nympho. She's the new eye-candy around here and the owners and everybody loves her. I mean she's like an Olympic acrobat specialist or something; the girl is bad.

"She was always at the top of her gymnastics class and she was the captain of her swim team."

"Oh, you know her personally?" Temptation asked.

"Yeah, that's my little cousin." Cognac answered.

"Oh I see the resemblance, nice asses must run in y'all family?" Temptation said, and giggled.

"Yeah, pretty much." Cognac replied, and smirked.

"Well, she's cool people. I try to look out for her and put her up on game and the way things go. These dudes are vultures around here. But look, Ima let y'all chill and Ima come back and holla at y'all before y'all go." Temptation said as she got up off of Devin.

"Okay." Cognac and Devin replied as Temptation walked away.

Nympho stepped up on stage and it was all eyes on her. She wore a white body suit with the ass out and multiple slits down the legs. She was the hottest thing going. The other strippers always pay close attention to her dynamic performances to up their game. Nympho seductively rocked her hips from left to right to the music. She started bouncing that ass and fiercely making it pop! They loved the way she was poking it in and out. The way her ass wiggled was breathtaking and made people fantasize of having a lick. She dropped that ass low for a second, bounced it then brought it back up and made it shake. She swiftly circled around the pole and then jumped up and grabbed the top. She flipped herself upward and did the splits on the ceiling, and made each as cheek jump one at a time. That move made about six or seven dudes immediately throw money on the stage! She acrobatically locked her legs tightly around the pole and then leaned back upside down slowly twirling around with no hands. She put her hands down on the stage and skillfully flipped over nice and slow landing in the splits. With one foot pointed north, the other south and her ass facing the crowd she undulated her booty as she looked back at the crowd. More people got up and tossed money on the stage, and others put it in the slits of her outfit. She bounced and popped that ass perfectly and then got up and grabbed the pole. She started making her ass clap, and bouncing it up and down. Devin was surprised when Cognac leaned over and told him that Nympho was her little cousin. The owners were very pleased as they watched from the side and behind the bar. Cognac was flabbergasted that it was her little cousin up there on the pole. However, what could Cognac say if she was in there enjoying the show her damn self. Nympho finished her set and exited the stage. Cognac leaned forward calling her name, grabbing her attention.

"Candace. Candace." Cognac called out trying to get her attention.

Nympho turned and looked to see who knew her by her government name. Her mouth dropped wide open when she noticed it was Cognac calling her. She walked over and sat next to Cognac looking slightly shocked.

"Candace...wsup girl?" Cognac asked.

"Nothing. What you doing here?" Nympho asked.

"I brought my boo here for Valentine's Day."

"Oh, okay." Candace replied.

"But I gotta ask, what are you doing working in a place like this?" Cognac asked.

"Pays the bills... but trust me I aint trying to make a career out of this." Candace stressed.

"Thank you." Cognac replied.

"Look, I'll be right back. I gotta go get something." Candace said as she stood up and walked away.

Candace took a few steps and turned around.

"Aye, Coney." Candace said.

"Yes boo?" Cognac asked.

Candace just looked at her for a second and then said "Don't tell nobody, okay?" Candace asked.

"I won't." Cognac replied as Candace smiled and walked away.

LATER THAT EVENING

Cognac and Devin sat on the couch in her living room sipping some Chardonnay. Slow jams played on the radio setting the mood just right. Cognac was laid back on the couch as Devin sat there gently massaging her feet. They were so pretty and Devin had a true foot fetish.

"Damn, you just don't know how bad I needed my feet rubbed." Cognac expressed as she enjoyed the blissful feeling.

"And you just don't know how much I enjoy doing it." Devin replied as he kissed her toes.

"You can't be kissing my feet like that." Cognac said, breathing a little harder.

"Oh yeah, why not?" Devin asked as he parted her legs and eased up in between her legs.

"Because..." Cognac replied, breathing sporadic, unable to complete her sentence.

"Because what, baby?" Devin asked, passionately nibbling her neck.

46   *Men-Tal*

"B, because...Oh shit...Oh shit...damn... You better stop." Cognac barely managed to say, seriously aroused by his every touch.

"And if I don't?" Devin asked, steady kissing on her neck, slowly grinding in between her legs.

"Oh Devin...shit baby, damn you feel so damn good. Ewww your dick is so fucking hard; I can feel that shit." Cognac uttered, loving the way Devin had then slid his hand down in between her legs, feeling all on her.

She was hot and wet as ever; at that point she would do anything he commanded. Her sexual utterances and whispers sounded good in his ears. He knew she was ready and loved how she could barely complete anything her horny ass tried to say. He gently raised her shirt, slowly rotating his tongue around her soft protruding breast and erect nipples. She rubbed his head, loving every bit of it. Endearingly he placed wet kisses on her stomach and asked "How about that?" Cognac sighed because his lips felt so damn good on her stomach. He climbed up a little further and started tenderly kissing her on neck. Cognac locked her legs around the small of his back and rubbed the back of his head. Breathing got heavier as he softly nibbled and sucked her bottom lip. That's such a stimulating aphrodisiac to her. They sensually French kissed; she could feel his hard dick pressing against her.

"Let's go get in the shower." Cognac said, looking him in his eyes with a grin.

"Let's do it." Devin replied.

Devin stood up and gently pulled her up and to him. They started kissing again as they made their way to the bathroom. She pushed him back up against the archway leading into the dining room. Kissing some more; she eased his shirt up and pulled it off. They moved towards the bathroom again and he eased her up against the table. He took her shirt off then unfastened her pants and pulled them off. He passionately squeezed, and felt all over and up in her ass crack. She loved being groped and manhandled by him. They moved into the bathroom and she put him up against the wall. She unfastened his pants and squatted as she pulled them down along with his boxers. She nibbled, kissed, and teased the head of his slightly salty dick as she completely pulled off his clothes and tossed them. She loved that nasty shit that people are ashamed to say that they like. She rose up and he turned her around putting her hands up against the wall. He kneeled down kissing all over her ass as he pulled off her clothes and threw them to the side. She leaned over turned the water on the perfect temperature. She went and grabbed a couple of wash cloths and towels from the bathroom pantry. When she turned around he was just standing there naked with a hard dick aiming to the left. She walked up to him and jacked him off for a second. She stepped in the shower and he stepped in behind her. He admired the way the water gorgeously cascaded over her figure. They joyfully washed each other very well. Bodies covered in suds; they hugged each other and kissed some more. Their slippery, soapy bodies felt so damn good as they hugged and kissed more, and more, and more. Feeling, and touching, he turned her around and she leaned forward. He kneeled down and with a face full of ass he ate her pussy from the back. The hot water felt so perfect washing up against her skin. His tongue felt incredible making her want to just explode in his damn mouth. She turned around and had him get up and stand under the shower. She admired and caressed his body with her hands as the water dripped down his frame. She kissed his neck, grabbed a handful of his dick and started stroking his shaft again. She kissed his chest and twirled her tongue around his nipple. She traced her tongue down his stomach. She squatted, lifted his dick and started licking it. She sensually sucked his balls like she was sucking the tender meat off of tasty neck bones. She stuck his dick in her mouth all the way to the back of her throat and held it there. She grabbed his hips and made him start fucking her in the mouth. His dick stood rock hard as fuck as she fiercely sucked, and sucked and fucking sucked. She had to force herself to stop sucking. She got up; they got out the shower and dried each other off. He took her by the hand and they went into the den. They walked over to the wide chase lounge chair in the corner. He sat down, laid back, and made her sit on his face. She held his waist and started riding his mouth. She stroked his dick as her sweet vaginal juices continuously seeped down his throat. She leaned forward and they passionately sixty-nined each other. She spit, slurped, sucked and gagged all on his dick. He gripped her fat ass and sucked her pussy making her toes stiffen and curl. The feeling was getting too intense; she couldn't hold it back anymore. She sat up and her body quivered as she came all in his mouth. She adored his solid dick and scooted down. She eased down on it and sighed as it slowly inserted her deeply. She rolled that ass all on his dick. He loved the way her ass looked as it pushed back and forth. He tried to think of anything to stop himself from exploding. He made her get up and turned around doggy-style. The way that ass spread as she arched it up was beguiling, and extremely enticing. He stuck his dick in and started breaking her off just the way she loved it. He pulled her hair and spanked that ass seriously. She moaned, and she screamed Fuck!! Damn baby shit!! She yelled his name as she came profusely!! He kept stroking that ass making it ripple like a fucking tsunami! That shit was looking so good like the XXX scenes in the nastiest porno flicks! He stroked, and spanked that ass harder. He clutched her hair, pulled out his dick and jacked the fuck out of it. He was so excited he shot cum all the way up her back and squeezed out the rest on her ass. She just looked back at him with the freakiest, stank look on her face like Damn nigga that shit was the fucking best.

FLASHBACKS AND NIGHTMARES OF AN INMATE

December 28, 2010, 12:36am... It was bedtime at the Wayne County Jail. The lights were out in a room overloaded with inmates, who were there for traffic violations, breaking and entering to convicted murderers awaiting trial. He couldn't believe that just hours ago he was a free man. He laid there in the top bunk all the way in the back of the room starring at the ceiling. He was straight trippin to his self that he was actually up in there. *This is some fucking bullshit. Why did I let this bitch get me up in here? Damn, I was fucking stupid. All of these other hoes out here I could've been fucking with...I should've just said fuck that bitch. Now she gone be out there fucking another nigga while I'm up in here with these hard leg niggas...I can't wait to get the fuck up out this bitch.* After while he started getting sleepy, and his eyes were getting heavy. Eventually he dozed off and fell into a deep sleep. About fifteen minutes later he was snatched out of the bunk by three inmates and thrown down on a mattress purposely placed on the floor in between the bed and the wall. He tried to get up and fight back but the reign of ruthless blows he suffered was too much for him to handle. The three inmates beat his ass and stumped him until he almost lost conscious and stopped fighting back. One of the guys grabbed his wrist tightly and held his arms. The other two dudes stripped his pants and draws off. He was petrified and delusional from the pummeling and the thought of being man handled like a little girl wrongfully taken of her virginity. His vision was hazy as he helplessly lied there on his stomach embracing what was about to traumatize him forever. Other inmates laid in their beds and looked on as they sodomized him until he passed out.

14 months later in Jackson Prison the traumatizing moment was still devastating to him. He contemplated suicide numerous times just never completely followed through with it. He would envision a sharp edged blade slicing clean through his artery... He didn't want to live with what had happened that night but fuck it he couldn't change the past. Unfortunately he was cursed to live with the haunting memories of that night

forever. Day after day he had flashes and nightmares that made him experience moments of insanity and show strange behavior. However...it had been a little over a year since the incarceration. Being locked behind bars like a caged animal can make a man lose his mind, and snap. He laid there on his bed daydreaming about that night at her house that got him sent there in the first place. He remembered so clear that fully loaded pistol in his hand and a heart full of hatred and rage. He rubbed the thin-lined keloid under his right eye from a blow he suffered during the incident. Just up the hallway you could hear the footsteps of a couple of officers approaching. They stood in front of the cell and looked at him.

"Alright, time to go." The officer said, unlocking the cell bars.

He slowly looked over at the officers as the bars were being opened and then sat up. Am I fucking dreaming? Am I finally out this muthafucka? It felt like this day would never come. Damn, it feels good to be free again.

FAMILY BRUNCH OVER UNCLE GARY'S HOUSE

2:00pm February 15, 2012 family members gathered over Uncle Gary's house for brunch. Gary's brother Calvin and his wife, Martha was over. Gary and his wife, Maxine was getting set to bring the food out to the dining room table. Regina was there being a huge help, assisting Uncle Gary. The doorbell rang and Martha went to the door to answer it.

"Who is it?" Martha asked.

"It's me, Rochelle, and Aunt Val." Cognac answered.

Martha opened up the door and let them in. They wiped their feet on the welcome mat and stepped inside. Valerie had a pleasant smile on her face and gave Martha a hug.

"How you doing, Martha? Good to see you." Valerie said as she coughed.

"I'm okay, Val. It's good to see you as well." Martha replied.

Cognac and Eric stepped inside and she shut the door behind them. She helped Valerie take her coat off so she could hang it up. Martha gave Eric and Cognac a hug and a kiss on the cheek. Eric took his shoes off, put them in the corner and handed his coat to Cognac. He walked in and was fully embraced with love.

"Hey, Aunt Martha." Cognac said, happy to see her.

"Hey, sweetie pie. How you doing?" Martha asked.

"I'm doing fine, Auntie. How have you been?" Cognac asked as she hung Valerie's coat in the vestibule closet just as you walk in.

"Well, I'm doing quite fine. Thank you for asking." Martha replied.

Cognac hung up her coat as well and went inside with the rest of the family. Cognac walked in the dining room where everyone was sitting and waiting to grub down on some delicious food. Calvin saw Cognac coming in and smiled.

"Is that my niece, Rachelle I see walking in here?" Calvin asked.

"Yes, Uncle Calvin it's me." Cognac replied as she leaned over and hugged him.

"Oops, wait a minute. What I meant to say is that my niece, Cognac walking in here." Calvin said, being silly.

Men-Tal

"Uncle Calvin, I see you feeling good today." Cognac replied with a smile.

"Yes I am. I'm feeling so good I'm about to get me one of them code names like y'all young folks." Calvin replied.

"What are you talking about, Uncle Calvin." Cognac asked as she sat down at the table.

"From now on you can call me Uncle Forty Ounce. If you Cognac then I'm Forty Ounce."

Calvin's wife, Martha looked at him like he was stupid and asked "Now why would you want to call yourself forty ounce? Don't you know you supposed to be setting an example?"

"I am setting an example. I'm setting an example for y'all old folks on how to step your game up. Y'all so old, withered up and decrepit you don't know how to keep up with the times." Calvin replied.

"But Calvin, you're older than everybody in here. So what are you saying?" Martha asked.

"Basically what I'm saying is the sixties are the new fifties, baby. I feel so good and young, later on I'm going to whoop Gary's butt on the pool table in the basement...and then Ima change my name again. You wanna know what Ima change my name to?" Calvin asked, being silly.

"No, but I'm sure you're going to tell me anyway." Martha replied, sarcastically.

"And unlike usual you are absolutely right, Martha. I'm changing my name to Metta Whoop That Ass World Peace." Calvin said, hilariously ignorant.

"Well Calvin, you might as well let your pants sag below your behind, show your drawls, and fix up one of them old school cars and put some of them super big rims on it." Gary said, sarcastically.

"Now I didn't say I wanted to go around looking ridiculous. These cars don't even look right no more after they put them big ole rims on it; it looks like their riding around in a damn chariot." Calvin replied.

Cognac just broke out laughing hysterically; she had to rub the tears from her eyes. Martha just looked at him like he was stupid and said. "Calvin...give it up. Shut up; I don't want to hear no more. I have spoken."

"I have spoken? Where you get that kinda talk from?" Calvin asked.

"Hey, you not the only one that learns from the youth; I got that from Cognac and them." Martha said with a smile, looking at Cognac, and gave her a high five.

Everyone was hungry and ready for some good eats. Calvin looked to the kitchen and said "Where is the food at? We're hungry out here." Gary walked out of the kitchen with a platter full of juicy grilled New York Strip Steaks. Regina walked out with a huge bowl of fluffy scrambled eggs with cheddar cheese all through it. Gary went back in the kitchen and brought out a tray of sliced turkey, turkey ham, and hash browns. Regina went back in the kitchen and brought out a huge glass dish of buttery grits.

"Now this is what I'm talking about! But where is the silverware and dipping spoons at?" Calvin asked, rubbing his hands together.

"Hold on Unc, we about to bring all of that out right now." Regina replied.

Gary brought out coffee, and orange juice and Regina brought out the Coffee-mate, a big picture of water and silverware. Calvin stood up and reached to dig in. Martha popped his hand and said "Calvin you know we supposed to say grace."

"Y'all people kill me always talking about somebody need to say grace before they eat. I aint never heard not one person ever say grace before they ate a candy bar. I never heard none of y'all hypocrites ever say grace before you grab a banana and eat it or drink a glass of Kool-Aid. I aint never seen nobody say grace before they drink water out of a nasty ass water hose. Y'all so far behind on saying grace y'all need to dedicate a whole day just to step ya grace game up." Calvin preached.

"Okay Calvin, to hell with the dang gum grace. You always fussin." Martha said as people chuckled and shook their heads.

Calvin closed his eyes and put his hands together and said "It's too late now so shut up; I'm about to say grace. Dear Lawd, please bless this food. Thank ya." Calvin said and opened his eyes and started digging in.

"What kind of grace was that?" Cognac asked.

"I don't know... an American grace I guess. God aint never said you had to have no special type of grace to eat. Everybody want to show off and act like they got the bomb grace to say to God that's gone get them on a fast track to Heaven. And then turn around and cuss folks out the rest of the day. Got road rage and hate to let folks over that got their blinker on when you diving." Calvin said as everyone just laughed and fixed their plates.

By that time somebody knocked at the door. Regina said she'll get it and went to the door. She looked out and saw that it was Reonna and Candace. She opened the door and let them in.

"Wsup late birds? We thought you weren't coming and just started to dig in." Regina said, hugging them as they came in and shut the door behind them.

"I hope it's some food left! You know Uncle Calvin don't believe in leaving no left over's." Reonna said, being funny as she took off her coat.

Regina laughed as she took Reonna and Candace's coat and hung them in the closet with everyone else's. They walked in and were greeted with love. They walked around the table hugging everybody. Candace and Reonna made their plates of food and sat next to Calvin and Martha. Calvin saw that Candace put her purse in her lap and wondered why she didn't put it on the floor.

"Candace, why don't you just sit your purse on the floor so you can be comfortable while you eat?" Calvin asked.

"That's bad luck, Uncle Calvin." Candace replied.

"Girl, you believe in that stuff? Remember this; superstition is only affective if you choose to believe in it. Trust me, can't no floor put bad luck in your purse or in your life. That's coo-coo to think like that." Uncle Calvin replied, looking at her while chewing on a mouth full of food.

"I here you Uncle Calvin but I remember one day me and my girl had walked out of this store. We split a pole on the way to the car. As soon as we pulled out of the lot a car crashed right into the back of us. What you got to say about that?" Candace asked.

"First let me ask do you believe in God?" Uncle Calvin asked, washing down his food with his drink.

"Yeah." Candace answered.

"Okay, well I guess you don't believe in using the spiritual logic that God gave you then. How you gone believe that God will save you from a devil but can't save you from a damn split pole? Where in the good book did it ever say that a split pole was gone getcha? Come on Na, you know how many times my wife done swept my feet? If that mess you saying was hardly true I would've been dead as a doorknob by now. Or I would've been throwing salt over my shoulder for the rest of my life. And I need that salt for my eggs and grits and stuff. Matter of fact pass me the salt please." Uncle Calvin preached ghetto sermon style.

"I know, you're right, Unc." Candace respectfully replied as she handed him the salt.

"So, Candace how old are you now?" Calvin asked.

"Twenty-one." Candace answered.

"I remember you were getting them good grades left and right in school. You were always on the honor role. I know you are a doctor or lawyer by now." Calvin said.

"Nall, I'm neither one of those. That's a little bit out of my league." Candace said and she ate a piece of steak.

"Oh, and I remember you was captain of your gym team. I thought you were going to be one of those Olympians running with that pole and leaping over the other pole." Calvin said, eating his food.

"Nall...I aint quite doing that either. Excuse me y'all I need to go to the restroom real quick" Candace said trying to get away from the spot light.

Candace stood up and mistakenly spilled her purse over on the floor. A few promotional flyers from Club Paradise spilled out visible where Calvin could see them. On the flyers was a picture of Candace standing to the side holding onto a pole in a swim suit. Calvin tried to help her pick the stuff up off of the floor and got a hold of one of the flyers.

"Good damn LAWD! I know my eyes aint that good but I can definitely see the girl on here got a tremendous ass. I mean gaud damn, Martha if you had an ass like this we would've had about several more kids." Calvin expressed with a stanky ass look on his face.

"Uncle Calvin." Regina said, surprised by his remarks.

Candace was completely embarrassed. She hurried up and grabbed her belongings off of the floor and darted to the bathroom.

"What? I'm just calling it like I see it." Calvin replied.

Martha grabbed the flyer out of his hand and looked at it and then blurted out.

"CALVIN, THAT'S CANDACE, YOUR NEICE YOU TALKING ABOUT LIKE THAT. But wait a minute, what is she doing on this stripper flyer?"

Everyone was shocked at what they'd heard. Reonna was extremely embarrassed as she sat there with her mouth open. She had no clue that her sister was a stripper. She took a deep breath then got up from the table and went to the bathroom to talk to her. Calvin couldn't believe it! He reached in his shirt pocket and grabbed his glasses and put them on. He grabbed the flyer back from Martha and looked at it.

"Aw Nall, I feel so terrible that I had to see this. I feel like I just got double the sin, because I lusted at the ass and it was my niece. AW HELL NALL, I feel dirty and nasty." Calvin said emphatically.

"Shame on you and you should feel dirty!" Martha said, popping him on the arm.

"Shame on me? It should be shame on her. Just because God blessed you with a big ass don't mean it was divine order for you to be a stripper and pole dancer. Why you can't be a teacher or a surgeon with a big ass?!" Calvin asked and continued eating.

"Man, just stuff your mouth with some food and shut up? It's like every word you say is making the moment worse. Candace is probably feeling terrible and humiliated right now." Gary suggested.

"Nall, what it is, is that the truth hurts and people don't like to hear it. People rather be pacified with a lie and pretend that they can't see the truth; same way folks do with religion." Calvin preached eloquently.

"Well aint nothing wrong with telling the truth but it is a proper way to say things to people. How would you like if I was to be truthful and tell you that you so black you still have a shadow at night? Or that your teeth so damn big that they look like two rows of Chiclets in your mouth or a pair of dinosaur partials? I don't think you would like that truth." Gary said.

"Uhhhh...who asked you? Why don't you take your fat ass in there and go prepare dinner?" Calvin asked and kept eating his food.

Reonna calmly knocked on the bathroom door. There was silence for a moment and Candace uttered "Yes?" Reonna asked "It's me, Reonna. Can I come in?" There was a brief moment of silence and then

Candace slowly opened the door. Candace leaned back up against the wall as Reonna entered and gently shut the door behind her. Candace was hoping her sister was not about to stress her about her lifestyle.

"You okay?" Reonna asked as she leaned back up against the sink.

"Yeah, yeah I'm cool...Just a little embarrassed. I guess you're about to let me have it, huh?" Candace asked.

"No, I'm not here to ridicule you about anything. I just really wanted to make sure you were okay." Reonna replied.

"Really? You stayed on my head about everything when we were growing up. You was worse than Momma." Candace respectfully said.

Reonna chuckled and replied "No I wasn't...or maybe just a little. That was because I only wanted the best for you. What else are big sisters for?" Reonna asked as they both chuckled.

"So, you really are not trying to interrogate me this time?" Candace asked with an eyebrow raised.

"No...SIKE HELL YEAH I WANNA KNOW. If you don't mind venting to me, what made you decide to be a stripper?" Reonna sincerely asked.

Candace slowly took a deep breath and excelled. "Pressure... I had just lost my Job for going off on my supervisor. He came on to me a lot and was sexually harassing me. I went off on him and told him I was going to report him and he made up a lie on me to his superiors and they fired me. They didn't even consider my side of the story. Eventually money got tight for me and I started struggling. I had bills coming up and no money coming in from anywhere else and I needed money ASAP. Then one of my girls who I was venting to asked me if I ever thought about being a stripper. At first I was like hell nall but then when she told me about the money I could make...I couldn't turn that down." Candace confessed.

"Why didn't you come to me, momma or dad for the money?" Reonna asked.

"Reonna, you know I don't ask y'all for money."

"Why, I'm your sister."

"It's just a habit. That one time momma tripped on me real hard over some money I owed her is why I don't ask. I was going to pay her but unfortunately I just didn't have it at the time. And I'm not saying someone doesn't have the right to come to you about some money when you owe them but she didn't have to come on me hard like she did. So now, I don't ask nobody for nothing."

"I understand how you feel, but you're supposed to be able to turn to me at least when you're under pressure."

"Yeah well, you got struggles of your own so I don't see how turning to you was going to eliminate my problems. I'm mean I had plenty of people giving me good advice but their advice didn't guarantee me a roof over my head at the present time. I had eviction notices, shut off notices, and repossession notices laid out on my table, and I was fucking hungry...I had to do something to keep a roof over my head." Candace said as her eyes watered as a couple of tears streamed down her face.

"Aw come here sis, it's going to be okay I promise." Reonna said as they hugged with Candace weeping on her shoulder.

SNAPPED

4:18pm A lady named Angela and her daughter, Marcena was at home talking in their kitchen. Angela was about to be heading out the door shortly to go have a business meeting with her girl. She was dressed sharp and classy; hair, and nails looking good. Marcena was standing at the stove cooking her cheese burger and fries. Marcena was young and beautiful like her mother. She had a nice figure just like her; curves and all, but just a smaller frame. Angela admired her daughter's looks; she just didn't want her growing up promiscuous like she did. Angela turned around and leaned back up against the counter.

"Cant nobody tell me you aint my child; you are the spitting image of me."

"I don't look nothing like you; I look just like my auntie, Jackie." Marcena said playfully.

"Duh, your auntie is my twin sister; thank you very much." Angela retorted playfully as well.

"I know, Momma; you are so beautiful, and I love looking like you. Matter of fact you are the better looking twin." Marcena replied, looking at her with a pleasant smile.

Angela smiled, thinking how she loves her daughter so much. "I don't see how you eat all that fattening stuff and maintain your shape." Angela said, shaking her head.

"All it is is a little cheese burger and fries." Marcena replied.

"Whatever, it's a fattening little cheese burger, AND FRIES."

"Momma, what you talking about? You used to eat like this and you still looking good. The men aint stopped hounding you yet." Marcena replied.

"Well, you don't want to have all this booty and thighs like I got. It's harder to maintain as you get older, and it gets you in trouble to." Angela preached.

"I don't know, I think I might like that trouble." Marcena said, jokingly.

"You know what? I don't want you growing up with sex and love being your main priority in life. You know you're nice looking but don't let nice looks and a nice body define your personality."

"I'm not Momma."

"I'm just saying because a lot of these nice looking girls grow up with a vanity filled heart. They figure because they look good that they're better than others. Some feel like because they have a lot of guys trying to holla at them that they can just treat a guy any ole kind of way. Many of them think the world is supposed to kiss their ass and just accept their smart mouths and nasty attitudes."

"Momma, you think I have a smart mouth?" Marcena asked as she grabbed a Tupperware bowl and put some paper towel in it.

"Yes you do." Angela replied with a straight face.

"From my lips to my hips yo I Get It From My Momma." Marcena said smiling as she looked back with her hand on her hips.

Angela was about to cut into her about her remarks when all of a sudden there was a knock at the door.

"You got somebody coming over here?" Angela asked with an incredulous look on her face.

"Naw." Marcena replied.

"It's probably Jehovah's Witness." Angela said as she headed to the door.

The door bell rang, and Angela said "I'm coming, I'm coming." Angela said, wondering who it could be.

Angela looked through the peep hole and was stunned. She aint seen this man in a year and a half almost, and definitely wasn't expecting him at her door step. She shook her head and unlocked the door. She opened it and looked at him through the screen door. He didn't look the same. He had a troubled look about himself. His hair was tacky, and his face was scruffy and unshaven.

"You just gone stare at me freezing to death out here or is it okay if I come in?" Marcello asked with a hard look on his face.

Angela took a deep breath then unlocked the door and opened it. Marcello knocked the snow off of his feet at the door and stepped in. The moment was awkward as they stood there looking at each other for a second. He glanced around at her nicely decorated home. Multiple statues and vases were in the living-room. Nice paintings hung from the walls. It felt good to be in a nice warm cozy home finally instead of a cold lonely cell. He was in a daze for a second and didn't hear Angela asking him a question. He rapidly blinked his eyes and shook his head as he regained focus.

"Hello, I'm asking you something." Angela said, waving her hand trying to get his attention.

"Oh my bad, my bad what did you say?" Marcello asked.

"I was asking when did you get out?" Angela asked.

"Today." Marcello answered.

"That's good. How did you get here?" Angela asked.

"I caught a ride and they dropped me off. I tried to call but your number isn't the same." Marcello said.

"I changed it two months ago." Angela answered.

"Am I interrupting anything?" Marcello asked as he looked around.

"Well, I am about to leave and go to a meeting. What happened to you, how did you get that keloid under your eye, and stitches on the other eye?"

"It's a long story I really don't want to get into right now. So, where's my daughter at?"

"She's in the kitchen." Angela replied.

Men-Tal

"I can't wait to see her. I hope she's happy to see me."

"I hope so to, but don't take offense if she's not though." Angela replied.

"Why you say that?" Marcello asked with a straight face.

"Marcello, you do know that the last time you've been over here to see her was two years ago, right?" Angela asked.

"Damn, I was locked up over a year. Y'all gone hold that against me?" Marcello asked.

"Even before you got locked up it had been a while since you showed your face over here. Your attention was completely focused on you and Ms. Rachelle or Cognac, whatever you want to call her, and not us." Angela replied, glancing back making sure Marcena wasn't listening.

"Damn, I just got out. Can you at least give me a break? Offer me a glass of water, juice; allow me to sit down and get warm or something." Marcello said with a slight scowl on his face.

"Look, I know I'm bitter about how you just abandoned us, but don't pretend like I don't have a reason to feel that way." Angela said with a serious face, looking him dead in his eyes.

"Look...you have no idea of where my head is right now." Marcello expressed, feeling sort of delusional, and spaced out.

"What's wrong? You look sort of lost or disturbed or something." Angela said, slight curious look on her face.

"Yeah, yeah, I'm alright." Marcello replied.

"You sure? You look like your mind is somewhere else right now." Angela pointed out.

"Look, I just got out okay... I mean...the things being locked up will do to you can make a man lose his sanity... Being caged and fed like an animal stripped of his freedom...gotta watch your back even when you're sleep. Look, I don't want to talk about it, I just wanted to stop by and see you and my daughter." Marcello said, taking a deep breath, trying to ignore the haunting thoughts of what happened to him when he was locked up.

"Okay well I'm sorry if I appear too hard or abrasive; my bad. Your daughter is in the kitchen cooking; follow me." Angela said as she turned and walked into the kitchen.

"Who at the door, Ma?" Marcena asked.

"I got a surprise for you." Angel answered as they walked into the kitchen.

It was a very dry surprise as Marcello entered the kitchen. Marcena wasn't expecting it to be her father as she did a double take.

"Oh...hey Dad." Marcena said, not sounding excited at all as she kept cooking.

"Hey sweetie." Marcello answered.

Marcello walked over and hugged her but the moment felt awkward and strange. Then he went and leaned back up against the counter. Angela thought what Marcena had on was inappropriate for the moment.

"Marcy, make sure you go put on some different clothes." Angela said.

"What's wrong with what I have on?" Marcena asked.

"Look, just do it." Angela said, not really wanting to go into detail.

"Okay, alright." Marcena replied.

"Well look you two; I have an important meeting I'm about to head out to. Marcello, I'm glad you're out and doing okay. Marcena, stay out of my liquor; I know you've been sneaking in it."Angela stressed as she grabbed her keys off of the counter.

"No I haven't." Marcena replied.

"Well, the ghost aint drink it, and I know what I drunk out of it. Now stay out of it and that's that. Now I gotta go, and I'll be back in a little while." Angela said as she kissed Marcena on the cheek.

Angela turned around and looked at Marcello.

"How long are you going to be here?" Angela asked.

"Only for a few; I just wanted to stop by for a brief moment. I have a couple of things I'm doing later." Marcello replied.

"Okay well I'll be back. Just call me later, and again I'm glad you're out." Angela said as she walked up front, grabbed her coat out of the closet and walked out the door.

Marcena was irritated and had a slight attitude because she felt like her mom was nit picking. She uttered to herself that her mom gets on her damn nerves sometimes and Marcello heard her say it.

"Dang, she gets on my nerves sometimes." Marcena stressed.

"Don't let it get you too bent out of shape, sweetie." Marcello said, trying to ease her thoughts.

"Whatever, I hate when she talks to me like I'm a little girl. She need to go head on with that mess." Marcena said with a snarl on her face.

"Yeah, but she's still your mother so you have to respect her." Marcello said humbly to his daughter.

"Dad, I got it." Marcena said with a little funky attitude.

Her attitude struck Marcello the wrong way. He couldn't help that part of him that just wanted to slap the attitude right out of her lil smart mouth ass. He remained calm and respectful; after all it is his daughter. He thought it out and calmly replied.

"Sweetie, I didn't come over here to be on a bad note with you. I did nothing wrong to you so your attitude aint called for. Besides I'm your father so you're supposed to respect me." Marcello said assertively.

"Father, huh? Maybe if you go back to where you was you wouldn't get my attitude." Marcena said disrespectfully as she exhaled very irritated.

"Okay...I don't know who the fuck you think you... You know what though? Calm all that stank attitude shit down because you pissing me the hell off." Marcello said with a serious look on his face.

Her telling him to go back to where he was caused him to think about that horrid place. He wanted to forget about it if he could but it's hard to do so when someone maliciously reminds you. He looked around trying to clear his thoughts. He noticed Angela's bottle of Ciroc on the counter, and grabbed a glass out of the cabinet. He poured him a nice amount and put the cap back on the bottle. Marcena turned around and looked at him. She gave him a nasty look as she watched him take a chug. Marcello shook his head and rubbed his eyes as he experienced vivid flashbacks of sodomy. He grabbed the bottle and poured him another glass.

"Didn't she say she didn't want nobody going in her liquor? She wasn't talking to just me." Marcena stressed very forward and disrespectfully.

So this little bitch gone keep disrespecting me like I aint shit? I was trying to be a good father but if you gone talk to me like I aint your father than fuck you...I aintcha father then. Ima treat you like one of these lil skank ass bitches in the street with all of that attitude shit.

Marcello swallowed the entire glass with some spilling down his jaw, and clothes. She had pissed him all the way off and pushed him over the fucking edge.

"So you just gone keep fucking disrespecting me?! You gone keep talking to me with that smart ass mouth like you grown?! You think you a grown fucking woman now?! You think you grown because these little punk ass boys done gassed your head up trying to holla at you?! I see you wearing them little skimpy ass fucking clothes trying to show your ass! You want to be a fucking woman?! You want to be grown and talk to a nigga with that fucked up stank ass attitude?! Well since you want to be grown, have a smart ass mouth, fucked up attitude, and show your ass Ima show you what the fuck all that get little smart mouth bitches like you. This is what a smart ass mouth and a stupid ass attitude get's you!!" Marcello yelled as he walked up on her unfastening his belt...

LOVE UNBREAKABLE

5:03pm Cognac unlocked the door and opened it for Aunt Val as she eased in the house. Cognac stomped the snow off of her feet and stepped in behind her. She helped Aunt Val take her coat off and hung it up. Cognac took her coat off and hung hers up as well. Eric came in last and shut the door behind him. He took off his shoes and practically left them in the middle of the floor. He didn't even take off of his coat and headed straight for the den where the video game was.

"Eric, what are you doing?" Cognac asked.

"About to go play the video game." Eric answered, pointing to the den.

"Eric, do you see how that video game makes you forget about certain daily practices you're supposed to automatically do?" Cognac asked.

"Like what, Momma?" Eric asked.

"Like taking off your coat and hanging it up when you come in the house and shoes in the middle of the floor. You know better. Now where does your coat and shoes belong?"

"I'm supposed to hang my coat in the closet and put my shoes together in the corner." Eric replied.

"Okay so come get your things, please." Cognac asked with a slight smile.

"Sorry Mom." Eric said as he walked over to get his stuff.

"No problem son, just want you to stay on top of what you're supposed to do." Cognac said and kissed him on the forehead.

Eric looked up at Cognac and said "You know what, Mom?"

"Tell me." Cognac answered.

"Before I play the video game, Ima read a chapter from my Egyptian History book Uncle Calvin gave me. I want to learn more about my culture and my other ancestors that hardly ever get talked about." Eric said.

"I like that Eric. If you do that I'll take you to the movies later." Cognac replied, proudly.

"Cool." Eric replied excitedly.

"Is your book outside in the truck?"

"Yes."

"Okay, go ahead and get it." Cognac said, unlocking the door with the remote.

Eric slipped on his shoes and walked out the door. Aunt Val looked on with a smile. She admired Cognac as a mother and all around person.

"I love you and that lil boy." Aunt Val said.

"We love you to, Auntie." Cognac replied.

"I know technically I'm your Aunt but to me you're the daughter I never had, and he the grandson I never had." Aunt Val said and slowly headed for the dining room.

Cognac's eyes almost watered when Val said that. She loved Aunt Val and would do anything for her. Cognac smiled as she watched Val ease into the dinning-room and sit down at the table.

"Lord have mercy, I'm so glad to be back home. I enjoyed having dinner and spending time with the family, but I was shole ready to go." Aunt Val said.

"Auntie, you know you love being over there. I think you hooked on Uncle Gary's good cooking." Cognac replied with a smile as she walked over and sat at the table as well.

Eric came back inside, put his wraps up and went to the den to read.

"Yeahhh I do love his cooking, but that Uncle Calvin of yours is something else. When he get to talking it's okay at first but after while he gets on your nerves."

"You talk like that aint your brother, Auntie."

"Yeah he is, but I had to disown him today after he practically got a woody from lusting after your cousin Candace." Val said, shaking her head pitifully.

Cognac laughed her ass off!

"Auntie, I don't think he knew it was Candace until he put his glasses on."

"Yeah, well his old behind need to sit his self down somewhere. Up here talking about these girls fat behinds. He's already walking a thin line, taking ninety-three different medications. If he actually gets a chance to really fill on one of them girls behinds for real he gone be pushing up daisies."

Cognac just chuckled at Val's remarks. She was sort of alarmed because Val had started coughing pretty bad. Cognac stopped laughing, concerned about how she was feeling.

"Auntie, how are you feeling?" Cognac asked with an eyebrow raised.

Val coughed again and replied "Oh I'm okay; it's just a little cold."

"Yeah, well I don't want that cold to get no worse. So you know what I'm going to do for you?" Cognac said as she walked over behind Val, wrapped her arms around her and kissed her on the jaw.

"Tell me what you're going to do for me." Aunt Val said with a pleasant smile.

"I'm going to go in that kitchen and make you some homemade chicken noodle soup."

"Oh yeah? How are you gone make it?" Aunt Val asked, placing her hand over Cognac's hand.

"The same way you taught me. Ima take a whole chicken, clean it and boil it in a big pot. Let the meat get super tender and then debone it. Then Ima chop and sauté some onions and garlic and put it in there. Then Ima chop up some fresh celery and shred some carrots and put it in there. And lastly Ima add a little salt and some pepper and let it simmer. Mmmm Mmmmm and you gone have the best tasting homemade chicken noodle soup of your life." Cognac expressed she stood up and headed for the kitchen.

"But wait aint you supposed to add noodles?" Aunt Val asked cleverly.

"Naw, you taught me to make my noodles on the side just in case I decide I want rice and chicken soup the next time." Cognac answered.

"You're going to be the perfect wife for someone some day. You remind me so much of your mother."

That subject touched Cognac and she walked back in the dining room and sat back down at the table.

"Auntie, was my mother a good mother?" Cognac asked.

"Yes, she was sweet and loving. She would hold you in her arms and sing you beautiful songs. She was very protective and nurturing to you... Hmmm... I remember that night she died in her sleep." Aunt Val said as she lowered her head, trying not to cry.

Cognac immediately felt compassion and said "Auntie, don't cry. My mother would be so honored to know how good you are to me and Eric. You're one of the best mother's anyone could ever hope for. And yes, I am that daughter you never had."

Val started crying and they hugged each other. Cognac's eyes watered and tears slowly trickled down her face as they held each other.

"I love you so much." Aunt Val uttered.

"I love you to." Cognac replied.

They stopped hugging and Cognac took her fingers and wiped away Val's tears. Val nodded her head and said "You are so good to me. I don't know what I would do without you."

"I don't know what I would do without you either. I do know what I'm about to do for you. I'm about to go in that kitchen and make you some soup with vegetables and herbs to help get rid of that nasty cough you got going on." Cognac said as she got up and walked to the kitchen.

Before Cognac stepped foot in the kitchen Val wanted to say one more thing.

"Rochelle." Aunt Val said.

"Mam?" Cognac respectfully turned around.

Val just looked at her with a sweet smile on her face and said "I'm glad God sent you to me."

Cognac just nodded her head, smiled and then replied... "Ditto" and then walked into the kitchen and made Val the best chicken noodle soup ever.

ANOTHER DAY IN PARADISE

10:49pm Nympho, Temptation and the other strippers were down in the basement of the strip club. Large mirrors and vanity were all around. The music was playing and they were partying. The house mom was selling stripper outfits, condoms, body spray etc and making a killing. The ladies were all talking shit, laughing loud, and trippin out. Weed smoke was the aroma in the air; it was a faint toxic cloud circulating the room. Temptation and a few ladies were dancing in the center of the floor. Most of the ladies were infatuated by Temptations humongous fat round ass. Two ladies, Nympho and Lexus had her sandwiched, freaking the shit out of her. Temptation flickered her tongue out of her mouth, brandishing her tongue ring. She bent over and touched her toes, wobbling her ass seductive as hell. Nympho was behind her smacking and squeezing her ass; she loved the way it moved and wiggled. She gripped her waist and started pumping her like she was fucking her doggy-style. Lexus stood in front of her griping here sides, and pumping her face; enjoying Temptation kissing and licking her pussy through her G-string. The other strippers were sitting around smoking, getting high as hell while watching the three way freak show in the center of the floor. After they finally finished fucking around Lexus stopped and went to freshen up. Temptation and Nympho finished messing around and went and stood off to the side and kicked it. Temptation leaned up against the wall, and lit a blunt.

"You know what? You're a cool muthafucka." Temptation said, taking a puff, and slowly exhaling smoke.

"Thank you boo. You cool peeps to." Nympho replied.

"You seem like you would be a doctor or a lawyer or something. What made you work here?" Temptation asked.

"Bills, bills, and more bills. I lost my job and started getting behind, and I didn't have any other income coming in so I came here. What made you work here?" Nympho asked.

"Money, sex, and mo money flat out. This is all I've ever done. I don't even know what it's like to work another type of job. They would probably fire me on the first day.

People wonder why I'm hard and callous like this. Hey... I was raped by both of my uncles when I was ten. I was raped by my step dad from age eleven to age fourteen. He would make me suck his dick and fuck him every day. He knew I was scared of him and he manipulated my fear. He told me if I said anything to anybody he would kill me, my mother and my daddy. One day he got killed by some niggas in the street. My mother made me go to his funeral and I spit on his bitch ass face while he was in the casket." Temptation said with a mean look on her face as she reminisced.

"Damn...that's deep. I'm surprised you don't hate working around men." Nympho replied.

"Girl, that shit don't phase me, my feelings are numb to these clown ass niggas. I don't give a fuck about them, their wives, their kids, none of that shit. I'll take their money in a heartbeat if their giving it up, and slit their throat in a blink of an eye if they try and fuck over me. Trust me." Temptation impressed.

"Wow, you should write a book on that shit. It would be a NEW YORK TIMES BESTSELLER." Nympho suggested.

"Yeah I've thought about it, and I still might. But look, it's time to go upstairs and get this money. Remember, niggas aint shit. It's all about money and power." Temptation stressed sincerely.

"Let's get it." Nympho said as she and Temptation walked up the stairs.

Strip club music and multiple shots of liquor had everybody's mind righteous. A slender stripper with hair draping down the middle of her back acrobatically twirled down the pole. Her well sculpted body looked like art as she gracefully worked the stage. The bartender poured ten shots of 1800 silver and placed them on the tray for the waitress. The waitress took the drinks over to a table full of ya average hood nigga's. A dude named Dre pulled out a wad of money, peeled off a fifty, and handed it to the waitress.

"I'll be right back with your change." The waitress said.

"Naw baby you good, keep that. Now what you can do since you so stacked and sexy is give a nigga a dance real quick." Dre said, lustfully starring her up and down.

"I don't give dances or none of that, I just serve drinks and food and that's it." The waitress replied.

"I hear all that baby, but I can give you so much more than what you getting just serving drinks and food." Dre said as he flicked through a thick stack of ones, fives and tens with his thumb.

"Trust me, I need money but Ima leave the lap dances and all that other stuff to the dancers. Ima stick with serving drinks and food. I make good enough tips doing this." The waitress expressed.

"Okay, no problem baby, but um...who is them chicks right there?" Dre asked and pointing.

The waitress looked and replied "That's Temptation and Nympho." The waitress answered.

"Oh yeah, well can you do me a small favor? And here's a tip for you in advance." Dre asked as he held up a fifty dollar bill.

"Um what's that for?" The waitress asked with a straight face, thinking to herself this nigga better not be trying to buy pussy from her.

"Calm down lil momma, I aint trying to come on you like that. Look, we celebrating with my boy, Marcello right here. He's just getting out today. So, can you tell them two ladies to come over here and can you bring us all two more rounds of that 18? And keep the change." Dre requested.

The waitress took the fifty and replied "I got you. I'll be right back."

The waitress walked over to Temptation and Nympho, said something and pointed at Dre and them. Dre and his fella's held their shots in their hands as Dre spoke.

"To my dude getting out today, it's good to have you home. May you live good and get mad pussy my nigga." Dre said as they toasted and downed their shots.

Temptation and Nympho walked up looking sexy and delicious.

"Wsup fellas?" Temptation asked with her big ass tits aiming right at Dre.

"Y'all wsup baby. I wanna get a dance from you and I'm wondering can ya girl hook my boy up with a dance. I'll definitely make it worth it." Dre asked, flashing a stack of one dollar bills.

The strippers set their money purses on the floor. Dre loved Temptation's thick fat ass and had her dance for him. Marcello was really digging how Nympho looked. She mounted herself on his lap and started riding him perfectly to the baseline of the music. Marcello placed his hands on her small waist loving her soft smooth skin. She had that Marcello spellbound as he looked in her sexy eyes. Her lips looked like they were dipped in honey, and tasted sweeter than Ciroc Peach. He loved the way her plump breast moved as she grinded on his hard dick. The waitress returned with their drinks and served them. The moment was so fucking surreal. They all toasted, slammed their drinks and kept the vibe going. Niggas was inebriated, vision was impaired, hazy and the music induced thoughts of sex and fantasy. Dre took handfuls of one-hundred dollar bills at a time and made it rain on Temptation and Nympho. Their booth was the livest booth in the strip club. All the other ladies wished they were over there getting that money. Marcello was looking at all the money Dre was tossing up and tip drilling. He just got out and he could've used that money and get out here and hustle with. However, all that money wafting down all over their asses made them work even harder. Nympho felt his hard dick through his cargo pants he had on. She turned around and rode his dick like she was trying to get pregnant. Marcello was getting horny as hell. He started squeezing on her ass but she didn't really give a damn about that. She leaned back on him and earned every Benjamin Franklin that floated down on her. Marcello started rubbing her stomach and talking to her in her ear.

"Damn, you sexy baby." Marcello said.

"Thank you baby. I heard you just got out." Nympho asked, spurring some of his thoughts.

Marcello started feeling weird like he was dreaming or something. He shook his head, and his eyes blinked fast as he tried to clear his mind. He replied "Yeah um...something like that."

Nympho sort of felt something wasn't right with him but she was blinded by the money. She brushed it off and kept dancing. Marcello had sporadic thoughts of that night that scarred his life forever. His breathing accelerated as he slowly eased his hand down to her pussy. She started feeling violated and moved his hand and kept dancing. Marcello envisioned himself fucking the dog shit out of her. He imagined his self pulling her hair and smacking the fuck out of her fat ass.

"I swear you look familiar." Marcello said in her ear.

"Oh yeah? I hope that's a good thing." Nympho said, thinking to herself that she had to leave soon.

"Definitely baby. You should come home with me tonight. I'll make it worth your while, sexy." Marcello said as he eased his hand down to her pussy again.

"Okay I'm done." Nympho said as she immediately got up.

"Damn, why you trippin?" Marcello asked with a scowl on his face.

"Nigga you trippin!" Nympho retorted.

Temptation noticed what was going on and stopped dancing.

"Wsup? What's the matter, Nymph?" Temptation asked, glancing at Marcello with a nasty look.

"Damn, wsup y'all?" Dre asked.

"This nigga disrespecting me." Nympho said.

"Braud, aint nobody doing shit to you." Marcello replied.

Temptation got up off of Dre and looked at Nympho curios as hell and asked "What he do to you?"

"He kept trying to stick his hand in my pussy, and I kept moving his hand off of me. Then he was trying to get me to come home with him." Nympho answered.

Dre and his other two boys tried to calm everything down before they drew too much attention.

"Look baby, we don't want no problems. We just here to celebrate my mans coming home. Can we just squash it, baby girl?" Dre asked.

"I'm good, I gotta go anyway. Matter of fact, I should've been left." Nympho said as she and temptation bent down and picked all the money off of the floor.

"You need me to walk you out?" Temptation asked.

"Naw I'm straight. I'm just parked in the back." Nympho answered.

Marcello experienced brief flashes of that night in the county. He shook his head and rubbed his eyes trying to shake those horrid thoughts. He looked over at Dre with an eerie look on his face and said "Aye, dog fuck this shit I'll be right back. I gotta hit the bathroom." Nympho shook her head as Marcello walked away.

"Aye, you sure you okay?" Dre asked Nympho sincerely.

"No I'm not, but I will be." Nympho answered.

"Aye Temp, I'm about go so just call me when you leave here." Nympho said as she looked at Temptation.

"Okay, be careful." Temptation replied as Nympho walked away.

Marcello was leaning over in the bathroom sink splashing water on his face a couple of times. He rose up and grabbed some paper towel from the dispenser. He dried his face and stared at his self in the mirror. He touched the scar under his right eye and had a flash of that night he was about to kill Cognac. His eyes fluttered as he shook his head trying to regain his focus. He looked at his self in the mirror and stared once again. He touched the stitches on the left side of his face. Immediately he had a flashback of when the county inmate punched him, knocking him dizzy just before they sodomized him. Marcello got angry and punched the bathroom walls a couple of times. Stupid lil bitch! Breathing heavily, he stared at himself in the mirror with a wicked scowl on his face. Some dude walked in to use the restroom. He looked at Marcello and thought he was kind of weird. He stepped inside the stall and looked back at Marcello just as he closed the stall door. Marcello went to the door and opened it. He looked to his right and saw Nympho walking out the back door. Marcello unnoticeably followed her. The surroundings in the back of the club were slightly raggedy. It was a nice size brick wall closing off the back lot. The lighting back there was half ass and her car was parked face forward in between the wall and another car. Nympho unlocked her doors with her remote, walked up and opened it. She was startled once she noticed Marcello standing there. What the fuck? Nympho stared at him, ready to defend herself if he tried something stupid. She reached her hand in her purse ready to pull her pistol if she had to. Marcello was off and wasn't any of that shit registering to him like it should've.

"I'm sorry if I offended you." Marcello said with a lost look in his eyes.

"Okay." Just get the fuck on. Nympho looked at him cautiously.

"Maybe I can buy you a drink or something next time." Marcello said.

Nigga hell nall! Nympho looked at him like he was out of his rabbit ass mind! "No, I just need you to leave me the hell alone. Okay?"

Marcello crazy self wasn't thinking she didn't want shit to do with his ass. He took offense to her reply. "Damn bitch, you aint gotta be disrespecting a nigga like that!"

Nigga you can't be serious! You got a lot of fucking nerve to call anybody disrespectful you ignorant bitch! Nympho just looked at him like he was nuts; like the ignorant fool he was in the club and replied. "Nigga fuck you!" Marcello was like fuck it, and walked away. She opened the door and got in her car. She sat her purse on the passenger seat. She went to shut the door just to find Marcello's hand immediately wrapped around her neck choking her! *Get the fuck off me you stupid mutha fucka! I hate you!* She was punching his arms and kicking him trying to get him off of her. She desperately tried reaching for her purse! He got his hand on it and they tussled with it for a second and it fell in the backseat. She managed to scratch the shit out of his face. Marcello grew vehemently enraged and snapped violently! He started punching her in the face, beating the dog shit out of her. *You sorry worthless bitch!* He grabbed the latch and let the driver's seat back. He was much too strong for her. His blows were far too much to bare and she was starting to fade. *Please somebody, anybody come help me.* Her vision got hazy and then she blacked out unconscious. Marcello smacked the shit out of her face and then just stared at her. He realized she was out of it, lifeless and vulnerable. He gently grabbed her face and sensually kissed her lips like she was his woman. He got erect and there was nothing stopping him from having his way with her. Quickly he unfastened her pants and pulled them off. He ripped her thong right off of her, and unzipped his pants. He opened her legs, pulled his dick out and then stuck it inside of her. He fucked her limp body for about five minutes. He made all kind of faces as he imagined himself fucking somebody else. In his mind the woman he saw was loving it! He started moaning and breathing heavily. Dammit you feel so fucking good...So... fucking... good. You like this shit? You like this shit don't you, you nasty bitch? His body started jerking; he couldn't hold it any longer! His eyes fluttered as he ejaculated all of his cum inside her. He immediately looked

Men-Tal

up and saw no one. He put his dick back in his pants, grabbed her sack of money. He swiftly went through her purse! What the fuck you got in here? Oh hell yeah, jack pot! He took her gun and got the fuck up out of there. Nympho was left lying in her car unconscious, bleeding and freezing. The parking lot security that was on the front side of the building during the scuffle. He just happened to cruise to the back of the building doing his normal half-ass routine. He looked around and didn't see anything wrong. He continued to cruise further and noticed Nympho's car door open. Curiously he peered at the scene and noticed her leg hanging out of the car. Immediately he whipped over to see what the hell had happened. He got out of the car and darted over and saw her beat up and naked. Immediately he took out his phone and called one of the owners. Frantically he told him what the hell had happened. The owner couldn't believe what the fuck he had just heard!! In no time the owner, the bouncer, and a few of the strippers came running out the back door! Temptation felt it in her heart that this shit wasn't good. Her heart damn near dropped when she saw them looking down in

Nympho's car. Oh my God, please don't let Nympho be dead she thought to herself as she fearfully walked over. Her hands trembled as she nervously covered her open mouth.

"Oh my God. Oh my God. OH MY GOOODDDDDD!!!!!!!" She yelled at the top of her lungs.

DETROIT RECEIVING HOSPITAL

11:48p.m. Cognac followed swiftly behind the paramedics as they wheeled Aunt Valerie into the hospital. She was on the phone with Regina letting her know what was going on. She kept it short and brief and then hung up as she walked through the entrance. The hospital staff had already been notified by the paramedics while in rout and they were expecting them. You could hear the paramedics saying Excuse us, coming through, coming through. They rushed Aunt Valerie to resuscitation unit immediately. The nurse was there awaiting Cognac to get Valerie's information from her.

"Hello, you're here with the patient?" Nurse Cassandra asked.

"Yes." Cognac asked.

"Okay, come with me." Cassandra said, leading Cognac to the family room.

They stepped inside and shut the door behind them. They walked over to the information counter. Cassandra walked around on the other side of the desk and sat in front of the computer. She quickly pulled up the data entry screen.

"Okay, what is the patience name?" Cassandra asked.

"Valerie Davenport." Cognac answered, feeling the anxiety building.

"What's her age?" Cassandra asked, typing all the information into the computer.

"Sixty-seven."

"Now I just need some medical history." Cassandra said, looking sharply at the screen.

"Okay." Cognac answered, nodding her head.

"Has she ever had a heart attack?"

"Not that I know of." Cognac answered, nervously tapping her finger on the desk top.

"Ever had a stroke?"

"Not to my knowledge."

"Has she ever had any surgeries?"

"Um...I'm not sure. I know not in her recent past." Cognac answered, looking around trying not to panic.

"Any other medical problems such as diabetes?"

"Yes."

"High blood pressure?"

"Yes."

"Any medications she takes?"

"I don't know the names, but I have her purse and medications with me."

Cognac reached in the purse and pulled out a few bottles of medications and hands them to the nurse. Cassandra input the information and handed them back to Cognac.

"Is there anyone you want us to contact for you?" Cassandra asked.

"I've already contacted my cousin, Regina. She should be here any minute." Cognac answered.

"Okay, well just have a seat and someone will be in here for you shortly."

"Okay, but I'ma step outside for a second and see if she is out there."

"Okay." Cassandra replied.

Cognac walked out of the family room and headed towards the entrance. When she stepped outside to call Regina she noticed Temptation. Temptation was leaned back up against the wall smoking a cigarette. Temptation had a stress look on her face and her nerves were bad. Cognac was surprised to see her and wondered what she was down there for.

"Hey, temptation." Cognac said as she walked over to her.

Temptation looked over and saw that it was Cognac and replied "Hey Cognac. How is she doing?"

It's impossible that you know that I'm down here with my aunt. You don't even know my aunt. With a curious look on her face she asked "How is who doing?"

Temptation was under the impression that Cognac was down there for Candace. She looked at Cognac sort of sideways.

"You know, your cousin, Candace." Temptation replied, wondering why she was acting clueless.

"My cousin, Candace? Why is Candace down here?" Cognac said with a bizarre look on her face.

Temptation took her last puff of the cigarette then dropped it on the ground and stepped on it.

"Oh, I figured somebody called you and told you and that's why you were here. Candace was beat up, raped and robbed." Temptation said, exhaling smoke.

"WHAT!!! Beat up and raped?!! OH MY GOD! When did this happen?! And where?!" Cognac asked, straight trippin!

"At the club. It was this guy that came up there with his boy's. One of his friends had just got out of jail and they brought him up there to show him a good time. They asked for me and Nympho, I mean Candace to come dance for them. She was dancing on the dude that had just got out. He started feeling on her, trying to get some pussy from her and she asked him to stop. He wouldn't stop and she got up and said she was done. The guy was a little salty and got up and went to the bathroom or something. Candace said she had to go, so she changed clothes and left. Right after that security found her in the parking lot unconscious. He fucked her up bad. Her face is real bruised, mouth busted and bloody, her pants were pulled off and she was laying there freezing. And that's when the club owners called the paramedics." Temptation expressed.

Cognac was straight flabbergasted. I got to be fucking dreaming. Wake up girl, this is only a dream. This aint happening for real. It has to be a dream. "No, no this can't be happening, THIS CAN'T BE FUCKING HAPPENING! I just brought my aunt down here because she couldn't fucking breathe right and was feeling weak. Now you telling my cousin was raped. What the fuck is going on?!" Cognac replied with a distraught face, starting to panic and pacing back and forth.

Cognac called Regina again. Regina answered and she informed her about what happened to Candace. Regina couldn't believe the shit she was hearing. You could hear Regina replying loud as hell! Cognac told her to call Reonna and tell her what was going on. Cognac told her she was about to go and check on Candace and to call her when she'd gotten down there. She hung up and she and Temptation swiftly went back inside. She had approval by the nursing staff to go back there and check on her cousin. She opened the door and she and Temptation quietly stepped in. The room was slightly chilly, and a TV was mounted in the upper corner. A huge picture window provided a vast view of the city and night lights. Multiple monitors and medical supplies were neatly in order. Cognac's heart thumped a little bit harder. The feeling was deep as she looked at Candace lying there all banged up. Tears instantly dripped down Cognac's face as she walked over to her. Candace was sleeping but woke up when she heard them. She could only look out the eye that wasn't swollen shut. Her mouth was fucked up, so she moaned sorrowfully as she managed to touch Cognac's hand.

"The doctor said her jaw was fractured, and it would hurt if she tries to say something." Temptation said as she compassionately looked on.

Cognac wiped her teary face as she gently placed her hand on top of Candace's hand.

"I love you, Candace. I hate this happened to you, and I promise Ima be here for you. Regina and Reonna are on their way. Aunt Val is down stairs being checked on by the doctors. I brought her here before I even knew you were here because she wasn't feeling too good. So, Ima go check on Aunt Val and I'll be back to check on you." Cognac said, and then turned and walked out the door.

Temptation followed out behind her and shut the door.

"Aye, Cognac." Temptation said.

Cognac turned around and answered "Hey."

"Those guys that came up there be up there often. That guy that had got out of jail they brought up there, I never seen him before."

"Did you happen to catch any of their names?" Cognac asked.

"Well, the guy I was dancing for his name is Andre, or some just call him Dre. The other guy, I think he said his name...was...Cello, or Marcello or something like that. I'm really not clear on that one." Temptation answered.

Cognac was instantly blown away by what Temptation just said. Marcello? She couldn't possibly be talking about my Marcello...could she? No, no Marcello's locked up.

Cognac had an incredulous face full of disbelief. "Wait, wait a minute, hold up... Did you just say, Marcello?"

"Yup, I'm about ninety percent sure that that is his name. What, you know him or something?" Temptation answered.

"Well, I used to date a guy named Marcello. He got locked up after he came in my house and tried to kill me and my son. The only thing that saved us was my cousin had come back over to get her phone. Luckily she saw his ass and she came out of nowhere with a cast iron skillet and cracked him in the face. It knocked his ass out, my son called the police and they came and picked his ass up."

Cognac expressed, trying to convince herself that it wasn't him.

"So that explains why he had that keloid under his eye!" Temptation replied.

"Which eye?" Cognac asked, mouth wide open.

"The right eye. He's a tall, stocky, light brown skinned guy with a little base in his voice." Temptation answered.

"No...Oh my God...I swear on my life he's gone pay." Cognac said, grinding her teeth.

"Oh my God! It is him, aint it?" Temptation replied slightly animated.

"Look, all of this is fucking me up right now. Plus I need to go check on my aunt and make sure she don't need anything or if they are about to discharge her. Take my number just in case you have to call me for anything." Cognac said.

Temptation pulled out her phone. "Okay, what is it?"

"It's three, one, three...five, six, six,..seven, one...thirty-seven."

"Okay, I'm locking it in."

"What's your number so I'll know it's you calling?" Cognac asked.

"It's three, one, three...seven, seven, nine...five, four, two, seven." Temptation said.

Cognac locked it in "Okay, I got it. So look, Ima go check on auntie and I'll be back up here."

"Okay, and I hope your aunt feels better."

"Thank you. I really, really appreciate you looking out for my cousin like this." Cognac said, hugging her.

"No problem. Go take care of auntie, and don't worry about Nympho, I mean Candace; I with her all the way."

"Thank you, and I'll be right back." Cognac said, turning around and started walking.

Temptation stood there and said "Aye..."

Cognac turned around and looked.

"He gone get what he got coming." Temptation said with a straight face.

Cognac nodded her head in agreement then turned around and left to go see how Aunt Val was doing and if she was being discharged yet. Cognac was still blown away and pissed about Marcello beating and raping Candace. She looked zoned out in another world as she walked pass the doctors and nurses. The hallways seemed to have a sickly stench in the air. On her way back to the family room she saw Regina signing in at the entrance.

"Hey, Gina." Cognac said as she walked up to her.

"Hey, how's auntie?" Regina asked as they hugged each other.

"I'm bout to find out if they said something yet. I was around on the other side checking on Candace. We gotta go in here in the family room and ask the nurse what's going on." Cognac said as they walked in the family room.

"How is Candace doing?" Regina asked, hoping for good news.

"She's messed up, Gina. The only positive thing about her situation is that she's alive." Cognac said, glancing over at Regina.

"Damn, she messed up like that?" Regina asked with a snarl on her face.

"He fucked her up, Gina, real bad." Cognac answered.

"Damn, I hate that. I wish I knew who it was because I would..." Regina said firmly before Cognac cut her off.

"You do know who it was." Cognac said.

"What?! Who?!" Regina asked with a serious look on her face.

Right when Cognac was about to tell her who did it they heard Dr. Robert Calvert say "Family for Valerie Davenport."

"Yes, right here." Cognac said as she and Regina approached him.

"This way please." Dr. Calvert said as they walked to the room on the right.

They stepped inside and Regina shut the door behind them.

"Is she ready to be discharged yet? I know she's gone have me running to the store to get her medicine. Then heat her up some of the chicken noodle soup I made her earlier." Cognac said, shaking her head and thinking how she was just ready to go home.

"Your aunt died from a stroke at twelve-fifteen a.m. I am so sorry for your loss. These things are very common for people of older age." Dr. Calvert expressed a gentle as he could.

"Huh?" Regina replied, hoping she heard wrong.

Please God, don't let him have just said what I think he did. Please just let me have heard him wrong. Please... not my aunt... "What? Wait a minute...she...she...oh my god this can't be happening. This can't be real. I'm dreaming. I know this has to be a nightmare.

Ima wake up soon. Ima wake up soon. Please God let this be a nightmare." Cognac said hysterically as she nervously backed up and sat down on the couch in disbelief.

Regina was in tears but a little more composed than Cognac. Regina sat down next to her and held her then placed Cognac's head on her shoulder. Cognac was shaking, her hands were trembling and her knees were knocking back and forth.

"Gina, tell me I'm just dreaming. Please tell me this is just a nightmare. Tell me auntie aint dead. I don't want her to be dead, Gina. Tell me she aint dead." Cognac pleaded so painful and helpless.

Regina just held her and rocked back and forth. Cognac wanted Regina to make this whole situation go away. A tear drop from Regina's eye dripped down on Cognac's face; it let her know that it was real...she wasn't dreaming. Aunt Valerie was pretty much Cognac's aunt and mother. Reality hit her hard and she started crying extremely like a child...who had just lost...one of the greatest loves she had ever felt.

WHEN WE SAY GOODBYE...

10:53a.m. February 20, 2012 at Elmwood Park Church of Christ... The day was quite gloomy outside. Burgundy and red fixtures adorned the off white colored walls of the church. A huge chandelier hung from the high cathedral ceiling proving a dim light. The preacher stood in front of chestnut colored wood grained podium giving his sermon. The family of Valerie Davenport sat along the front row of the church. Teary faces, sniffles, and scattered cries made the moment heartfelt and sorrowful. The preacher spoke compassionately to the family and those attending service. On the left side of the casket were two beautiful bouquets of flowers. One bouquet represented Valerie's brothers and sisters, and the other representing the In-Laws. On the right side of the casket were two more bouquets of flowers. One of the bouquets represented the grandkids, nieces and nephews and the other representing the church and close friends. Cognac was doing her best to hold herself together. Damn, it's so hard to say goodbye to one you love so dearly. The service was full of sad songs and scripture readings but like everything it was coming to an end. The preacher asked the Pallbearers and Flower bearers to come forth. It was a struggle for Cognac to hold it together as she looked on, slightly rocking back and forth. The usher handed the flower bearers the flowers as they proceeded to the left side. Another usher had stepped to the casket after they had removed the flowers that adorned it. She unfolded the cloths and placed them neatly in the casket. And the moment came...when Cognac had to close her eyes tightly...she sniffled as streaming tears dripped down her saddened face... She did not want to see the usher grab the handle and shut the casket.

11:23a.m. Elmwood Park Cemetery... The scenery couldn't have been more disheartening. The sky was cloudy and gray with no sunshine. The trees were bare, wet and brittle. Snow flurries fell upon the ice cold ground that yielded no cushion to the feet. Family members and a few friends gathered under a small tent. The closed casket was centered in the middle with the flowers on top. The preacher had everyone close their eyes and bow their heads. They prayed with positive thoughts and energy as they wished Valerie a beautiful afterlife. After the prayer they sang two songs. Her son Eric was sitting next to her with his arms wrapped around her. He had a face full of tears and couldn't stop crying. It was time to conclude the burial service so the preacher gave his final remarks and blessings to the family. A representative of the funeral home gave his consoling remarks as well and then they respectively departed. Cognac couldn't believe that this shit was real. She had just cooked chicken noodle soup for Valerie and had a very heartfelt conversation with her a few days ago. Black teardrops trickled down her face as she put on her large sunglasses. Eric's father who also attended the service had little Eric ride back with him to the church. He wanted to talk with him father to son and make sure he would be okay. Regina walked over and put her arm around Cognac. They went and got back in the limo and then headed back to the church to have dinner. As they drove back Cognac gazed out of the window with a blank stare. She cried silently to herself, often sniffling with a face full of tears. I promise I will never forget all of the pleasant smiles and laughter we shared. All the times you had me in the kitchen with you teaching me how to cook... Maybe now you're reunited with your husband now in another life... Oh how beautiful it will be to see your beautiful face again...one day...I love you and miss you.

AN IDLE MIND IS...

Some say an idle mind is the devil's playground...and if that be so then a dangerous mind is his most hostile killing field and abode. However...Cognac sat at her dining-room table, thinking. Why is all this stuff happening to me? What type of sin could I have possibly committed to have to embrace such ongoing drama? She had been sitting there for hours zoned out and contemplating. Devin had been trying to talk to Cognac and help ease her mind. It can be sort of hard to support when the one you love has been giving you the cold shoulder. Cognac hadn't been very talkative since the night Aunt Val died. Devin walked up to Cognac, pulled out a chair and sat down.

"Baby, do you need anything?" Devin asked.

Cognac continued her blank stare off into the living room and shook her head "No".

"I know it's tough for you right now and you don't want to talk. Ima just ride over to my house and make sure everything is cool.

Ima grab a couple of things and some work clothes and I'll be right back okay?" Devin said.

Cognac never looked at him, just remained silent for a brief moment and then replied "I just want to be alone right now."

Devin was a tad bit surprised by her response towards him. He knew that she had been going through a lot but didn't think she needed to respond like that. Over the last few nights Cognac had been strangely leaving out and not coming back for hours. Devin would call and she wouldn't answer. As un-thoughtful as it may sound Devin was starting to wonder if she had been going out and seeing someone else. Hell, she was giving him a serious cold shoulder.

"Ooookay... Ummm, I hope that this isn't inappropriate for me to mention right now but... You have been a little extra standoffish towards me these last few nights and you've been leaving out late and not coming back for hours. I call you and you don't answer your phone. Normally when I call you and you're around your girlfriends or family you always answer. Which leads me to the question have you been out confiding in and seeking comfort from someone else?" Devin respectfully asked.

Cognac took a deep breath, lowered her head. She covered her face with her hands and rested her elbows on the table.

"I just want to be alone."

Devin snickered at Cognac's bleak response and replied "Hmm, I guess I'm right... And as you wish I guess I'll just leave you alone." Devin said as he got up.

He put the chair back under the table and then went and got his coat out of the front closet. He put it on along with his hat and left out, shutting the door behind him. The house was silent and lonely. In her solitude she pleasantly embraced her rage and inner demons. She discarded all thoughts of righteousness, forgiveness, and religion. She finally got up and walked into the kitchen. She grabbed a small crystal glass out of the cabinet. She never uses those glasses unless it was a special occasion. She had a brand new frosty pint of Hennessey out of the freezer and poured her some. She took a real nice swallow and then looked inside the glass. She looked at her reflection rippling on the surface of the liquor. She saw the side of her that really didn't give a fuck. She walked

Men-Tal

into the bedroom and sat her drink down on the nightstand. She went in the bottom drawer of her dresser and pulled out a silver case. She sat down on the bed and laid the case on her lap. The case had a key safe lock on both sides. She put in the code 1993 on both sides and unlocked it. She opened it and behold; her beautiful, shinny pistol. She took the pistol out and the clip that was on the side and sat the case on the bed. She sat the gun and the clip on the bed as well. She opened the bottom drawer of the nightstand looking for the case of bullets but only found folded shirts. She flipped through the shirts and still, no bullets. She closed the drawer and walked over to the chestnut colored armoire and opened the door. Jewelry, tampons. Where the fuck did I put that case of damn bullets? Cognac's eyes quickly scanned the hell out of those shelves flipping through different things. Oh, I know. It got to be down here! Cognac squatted down and opened the top drawer. She paused for a second and tried to remember. Oh yeah she flipped over the clothes on the right side of the drawer and bingo! Found it! She picked up the small case and the key laying next to it. She unlocked the case and opened it. Inside were all the bullets she needed to let off her violent fury and rage. She sniggered and shook her head in disbelief as she loaded bullets in the clip. This nigga gone rape my little cousin? I got something for that ass. She popped the clip in the pistol and cocked it. Yeah. She took a sip of her drink and aimed her pistol at the mirror. She admired how she looked holding the pistol with one eye closed. Ima show em what a real gangsta bitch look like. She was a sexy black woman in a black dress. She wore a large black Panama Swinger hat while holding a pistol with no heart. "You gone die tonight." Cognac said as she swallowed the last of her drink. She looked down at herself and thought; grabbing her dress while asking herself hold up; what the fuck are you going to do to anybody wearing a damn dress? Gotta change out of this before I go anywhere. As she went to change into something more suitable she thought about Devin; she hated that he felt like she was up to something; it troubled her because she loved him. However, him finding out certain information may have come at the expense of his life. She didn't want anyone to know what type of mission she was on. So therefore she didn't tell him that she was stalking Marcello when she was leaving out each night. She rode by a couple of spots but never saw him. She knew the police was looking for him for raping Candace. She also knew that he couldn't be at his mother's house because that's the first place the police would go. He couldn't be at Andre's house because that's the second place they would look for him at. He had a few other spots that he could possibly be hiding out at that she knew of. There was one particular spot she was practically sure that he could be at. A place where the entrance and exit was dark and secluded. A place where not many people would be and was trust worthy...the basement of his boy's bar downtown. He'd taken her there a couple of times before. Plan A was simple; wait till after club hours and coast was clear. She'd pick the lock on the back door as long as it wasn't too difficult. She'd sneak in and then bang his ass and his boy's ass with every round in the clip. Afterwards make sure that the coast was clear and make a clean get away. Bottom line Marcello was marked for death and the reaper was coming for him.

DOUBLE SHOT OF RED RUM

February 21, 2012 Downtown Detroit MI. 3:15a.m.   At this point Cognac was operating off of pure rage and revenge. It was very dark wet looking behind Lake's Bar. Her anger and emotions basically blinded her to the level of danger around her. She had never done anything like this before. However, she was operating off adrenalin and hate, and didn't give a damn about karma, repercussions, jail time or danger. She was just about to do her impersonation of a lock-smith and pick the lock if she could. Just as she got ready to stick in she stopped, and listened... Shit! She heard someone talking while approaching the door. She quietly eased back, placing the lock pick in her coat pocket. She grabbed her pistol out of her pocket, holding it tightly with both hands. She looked closely as the door unlocked and opened. Don't get nervous; just bust his ass in the head and run. With her heartbeat accelerated and her finger on the trigger, she was about to blow Marcello's head off. It wasn't him though; it was somebody else. Shit, it aint him! A dark skinned dude stepped out and walked to his right; he didn't even see her. He was too busy running his mouth about something that just happened. He had no clue that Cognac was behind the door.

"I'm headed to the car right now. Where you at? I did that shit already. Now it's time to shoot this move so we can get that bread." Phillip said, walking swiftly to his car.

She couldn't make out the rest of the shit he was saying as he walked off. That's right, just go ahead and leave before I have to blast yo ass to. Nevertheless Cognac's mission just got that much easier. Hell yeah, I aint gotta try to pick this damn lock. I hadn't done it in a while anyway. She desperately grabbed the door handle before it closed. She figured that must have been the owner leaving out for the night. Looking at ole boy she quickly stepped inside. She vigilantly looked around as she shut the door quietly. She was in a dark hallway. She could either walk forward which led to a door that opened to the bar, or she could walk down the basement stairs to her left. She decided to peek through the window of the door and see if anyone was in the bar. She quietly eased forward; there was a men and women's bathroom to her right. She listened to see if she heard any voices. She proceeded and looked through the window. No sign of his ass or anybody else. It was just an empty bar and all the tables and liquor seemed to be in place. She quietly made her way to the other side and down the stairs. The lights were on yet it was silent; she hoped it wasn't nigga's awaiting her with pistols. Damn, what if this nigga aint even here? She'd come too far to turn back though; at least it was worth the look. She held onto the loose railing trying to be as quiet as possible as she stepped down. She wasn't actually sure if Marcello was there or not; she just knew that he laid low here before. She looked around and saw no one. There were a couple of couches with cocktail tables in front of them. She squinted her eyes as she unknowingly stepped in front of a movie projector playing a violent gangsta film on the big screen just behind her. She held her hand up and covered her eyes from the blinding light and stepped out of the way. She looked further back and saw a door on the right; it's probably just a bathroom or a room full of junk or something. To the left was a door almost halfway opened. She curiously peered closer and wondered what was back there. With a mean scowl on her face she walked to the door. She listened closely and heard nothing. She carefully peeped in... she saw part of a pool table. She peeped in a little more and saw someone's shoe and leg. What the hell? Is someone laying on a pool table? I know this his punk ass! Redemption for her and her family was just beyond the door. She swiftly opened the door and pointed her gun. She gasped for breath harder than she had ever done!! Oh my God... Her eyes bulged with fear and disbelief!! Her heart pounded like she was about to go into cardiac arrest. Her body felt hollow and lifeless. Marcello? He was laid back on a pool table with a bullet hole in his head and blood spilling down his face. His eyes and mouth were wide open. She had never seen a frightened look on his face like that before. He had been shot twice in the chest and his shirt was bloody as hell. She couldn't believe she had just walked in on a murder scene. Now everything was slowly starting to come together. She understood what ole boy was talking about when he walked out and said I just did that shit. She figured ole boy must have killed him, but why would he just leave him...if he wasn't coming right back? Cognac thought about it for a second, immediately got nervous and looked around. She heard a car door shut just outside and then the back door opened!! Oh my God I'm so sorry for trying to do something so stupid. Please get me out of this. I don't want to die. I don't want to die like this. She got so fucking scared as she heard a couple of people coming in and walking down the stairs. She didn't know what to do! She could either start blasting now or soon as they come through the door.

"So you laid that nigga out, huh?" Edward asked as he and Phillip walked to the back room.

"Like a muthafuckin door mat. One to the head and twice in the chest; piece of cake." Phillip responded.

"Hell yeah, we gone be fucking filthy rich!" Edward said, excitedly.

"I could've sworn I pulled this door up closer than this." Phillip said with a puzzled look on his face.

"Man, I hope this shit aint got you losing your mind!" Edward said, slapping Marcello on the side of the leg as he walked up and looked at him.

"Trust me, I aint. I just want to knock this shit on out and go bury this nigga." Phillip said, walking to the closet and grabbing the chainsaw.

Cognac hid on the floor up under the bar just feet away from the pool table. She was scared for her life, and couldn't believe this shit was happening. She was trying not to breathe loud at all. She prayed no one walked back behind the bar. If they looked down under the bar they would definitely see her. She knew if they found her that it was a wrap. They would put a bullet in her head and bury her with Marcello.

"Damn, that's a big ass chainsaw! What are you finna do with that?" Edward asked.

"Surgery." Phillip replied very cut and dry.

"Damn nigga I feel you. Hell yeah!! Show me the money baby!!" Edward replied emphatically.

"Aye, can you grab that extension cord from behind the bar?" Phillip asked.

Cognac heard him ask him to walk back there, and got scared as hell! Please God don't let him see me. Edward walked around the bar and half-assed looked on the lower shelf.

He was intoxicated and wasn't paying attention.

"I don't see it." Edward said, looking around.

"Maybe if you turn the light on you will see it." Phillip said sarcastically.

Edward looked up, pulled the light switch and said "Nigga, the light bulb don't even work. Where are some more light bulbs at?"

Cognac laid on the floor trembling, doing her best to hold it together. She took deep, slow breaths as she hoped for a safe escape. Her pulse accelerated as she looked at Phillip's feet as he walked back behind the bar to get the cord his self. Phillip reached up and screwed the light bulb in a little tighter. He pulled the switch and the light came right on.

"Whatever nigga." Edward said and walked back over by Marcello.

"Here go the damn cord right here on the floor on the side of the bar. All you had to do was just look." Phillip said as he walked over to the right side of the bar and picked up the cord.

Cognac's heart was beating like she had a Red Bull energy drink and cocaine! She exhaled a little easier once Phillip walked back over to the pool table. Phillip plugged the cord into the wall and then plugged up the chainsaw.

"Aye, grab the trash bags from behind the bar. I know for a fact there behind there because I just put them back there earlier." Phillip asked.

"I better look on the floor this time before you have me on a wild goose chase again." Edward replied sarcastically.

Cognac heard them talking and just knew Edward was about to see her. Edward walked back there and looked around. He saw them on the top shelf, grabbed them and walked back over on the other side. Before they could follow through with the plan they heard someone ringing the bar doorbell. They inquisitively looked up at each other thinking who it could be!

"Damn, who the fuck could be at the door right now?! Don't they know it's after business hours?!" Phillip asked, heart thumping.

"Shit, did you have somebody coming through and you just forgot or something?" Edward asked with a face full of panic.

"Hell nall nigga I aint slippin like that...but we better check and see who the fuck it is though." Phillip said as he pulled his pistol from the small of his back and cocked it.

Phillip and Edward walked up the stairs to see who was at the door. They had mean scowls on their faces as they looked around. Edward pulled his pistol out as they approached the door. The doorbell rang once again, and Phillip peeped through the peephole.

"It's the PoPo's. Put your gun up and act like you're cleaning up before we leave." Phillip uttered as he tucked his gun back in the back of his pants.

Phillip glanced around real quick, opened the door and respectably addressed the two officers.

"Hello gentlemen, can I help you." Phillip asked.

"Yes, we were informed that there were gunshots fired in this area. Have you heard anything?" Officer Wiggins asked.

"No, I haven't heard anything outside of the usual." Phillip replied, heart thumping hard as hell.

The officers were sort of suspicious but didn't ask to come inside and take a look around.

"Okay, if you see or hear anything call us." Officer Willis said and then left.

"Absolutely, will do." Phillip answered.

The officers turned and walked away and then Phillip shut the door. He took a deep breath and exhaled with great relief.

"Dog, this bitch better definitely come through with this money. Sheiit we was close as fuck to getting life in prison just a minute ago." Edward said, trying to calm down.

"Hell yeah so come on lets go get this nigga up out of here before they asses get suspicious and come back." Phillip said.

While they were up stairs answering the door Cognac had decided it was time to make a move. God please let me make it out of here alive. I swear I will never do this again, EVER. She cautiously eased up and peeked around the bar making sure the coast was clear. She covered her mouth, trying not to be heard crying. She swiftly walked out the room as quietly as she could. She nervously aimed her pistol as she carefully approached the staircase. She eased up the stairs with her back to the wall. She peeped around the corner as she made it to the backdoor. The coast was clear so she opened the door and ran for her life. It seemed like she couldn't make it back to her truck fast enough! A black car pulled in right behind Cognac. Cognac damn near panicked and shitted on herself because she was so scared. She calmly shut the door and then looked in her rearview mirror. She thought that it was the police pulling up behind her. The lady that was driving looked over at Cognac as she eased pass. Cognac looked her right in the eyes and quickly looked away. Girl, come on stop fumbling these damn keys!! Cognac's hands trembled as she started the ignition, backed out and quickly pulled the hell off. By time Phillip and Edward made their way back downstairs Cognac was up out of there. Phillip felt a cold draft as he opened the door as he entered the hallway. Surprise and anger was written on his face once he noticed the backdoor was opened. He drew his pistol who ever the fuck in here is about to get fucked up! Edward pulled his pistol out as well as they vigilantly approached the door. With gun aimed Phillip opened up the backdoor all the way and carefully peeked out. He looked both ways and saw nothing.

He shut the door and locked it. He twisted the knob and saw that it was secure; there was no sign of forced entry. Damn...how the fuck did this door get opened? I know I'm not crazy and left this door open like that... He asked Edward if he recalled the door being open. Edward told him he didn't think it was. Phillip shook his head and they cautiously eased down the basement stairs. Nothing was different as they looked around and ready to blast any muthafucka on sight. Phillip listened closely as they cautiously moved to the backroom. Edward went and checked the room on the right; it was nothing there but a bunch of junk and stuff for the club. Edward swiftly went back on the other side with Phillip. Phillip just knew they were being set up! He immediately kicked the door wide open, pointing his pistol with his finger on the trigger! He saw no one but a dead ass Marcello. Phillip figured the only place somebody could be hiding at was behind the bar. He waved his hand for Edward to go around the left side of the bar. Phillip leaped up on top of the bar with his gun aimed down but saw no one. They were both confused and Phillip jumped down scratching his head.

"What the fuck?" Phillip said as he glanced around.

"How was the door open if nobody came in and aint nobody here?" Edward asked with a mean puzzled look on his face.

"I don't know; I can't even think straight right now." Phillip said, shaking his head.

Edward looked down on the floor and asked "Who big ass hat is that?"

Phillip looked down and then picked it up. He looked at it real good and replied "I don't know. It's probably ole girl's hat. We gotta find out how that door got open. I know for a fact that door wasn't open when we walked up there."

Phillip said as he sat the hat down on the bar and walked on the other side. He shook his head and then his cell phone rang. He looked at it and saw that it was Nook-Nook calling him. He answered "Wsup baby?"

"I'm out back. Come open the door for me." Nook-Nook replied.

"Alright, here I come." Phillip said as he hung up the phone and headed up stairs.

He looked through the peephole and then opened the door. Nook-Nook stepped in looking like a sexy ass Dime Diva. Dark brown stretch pants, dark brown boots, and a waist length dark brown leather bomber coat. She shut the door behind her and then pulled him to her and kissed his lips. She was the aggressive type; she takes whatever she wants.

"You handle that?" Nook-Nook asked.

"Yeah." Phillip replied sort of dry.

"Where is he at?"

"Downstairs in the backroom."

She walked down the stairs and spoke to Edward as she proceeded to the backroom. She opened the door and saw Marcello dead as a doorknob.

"You got exactly what the fuck you deserve you scandalous bitch." Nook-Nook said with a sneered look on her face.

She walked back in the front room and looked at Phillip and said "Good shit. Y'all about to dump him?"

"Yeah, but first we gotta little problem." Phillip said.

"What's that?" Nook-Nook asked.

"Somebody else was here." Phillip answered, tucking his gun back in his pants.

"What you mean?" Nook-Nook asked with her mouth opened.

"I mean literally just that; somebody was here." Phillip replied.

"Okay did you see somebody?" What makes you say that? Did you shoot at them? Tell me something." Nook-Nook said, trying not to get frustrated.

"No, I didn't see anybody. Me and Ed were about to bag ole boy and get him up out of here. We heard the doorbell ring. We went upstairs to see who it was and it was the police. They were saying someone reported that they heard gunfire and seeing if we heard anything. I told them nall and they left. We headed back down here and when we got to the door it was partially open." Phillip explained.

"Well, you know it wasn't the police because y'all asses would be arrested right now. Maybe y'all just left the door open by mistake." Nook-Nook suggested.

"Aye y'all, fuck all this chit chatting, we gotta dump this body before the five-O decide to come back up over here." Edward said.

"Hell yeah, let's knock that shit out." Phillip concurred.

"Okay, well y'all call me after y'all finish." Nook-Nook said and headed for the door.

Phillip grabbed the black swinger hat from off of the bar and looked at Nook-Nook.

Men-Tal

"Aye, why don't you take this big ass hat with you?"

"What you giving me that for?" Nook-Nook asked as she took it from him, looking at it.

"I don't know. I didn't know if it was yours or not. Just throw it out when you leave." Phillip answered.

"I aint bout to throw it away; this hat brand new and fly as fuck...and I've been looking for a hat like this and aint been able find it nowhere. Besides...I'm sure it will look sexy on me." She said, putting the hat on, cocking it to the side and went and looked at herself in the mirror.

"Yeah, you do look sexy than a muthafucka right now." Phillip replied, looked her up and down.

Without even looking at him she replied "Get your nasty eyes off of my ass and finish the job, please?

Nook-Nook walked up the stairs and out the door. As soon as she stepped out she heard police sirens. Her heart almost jumped through her chest! She exhaled when she noticed they darted pass on their way to handle another problem. She took that as a sign and immediately got in her car. She adjusted the rearview mirror and looked at how she looked with the hat on her head. She then took the hat off and tossed it in the back seat, started her car and pulled the fuck off.

SECRETS MUST BE BURRIED IN TRUST

February 21, 2012, Tuesday 7:47a.m., Essential Beauty Salon... Regina, Benita, and Peaches were blown away by what Cognac had just told them. Regina was sitting on the couch to Cognac's left. Benita and Peaches were sitting in foldout chairs in front of the couch. With mouths wide open they sat there momentarily speechless.

"Oh my God... I can't believe that Marcello was that damn crazy. And then to walk in and find him dead is absolutely devastating. I know you're shaken up and I just want you to be okay." Regina said very concerned.

"I swear I got your back if anything goes down." Peaches said, sincerely.

"Do you need us to do anything?" Benita asked.

Cognac somewhat shook her head and replied "I don't know...I just need y'all to keep being in my corner like always. I'm just scared right now." Cognac answered.

"Well we definitely got your back. We're in this together." Regina impressed.

"So um, did you call the police?" Peaches asked.

"No, I can't." Cognac said as she looked up at her.

"Why not?" Peaches asked with a confused look on her face.

"Because, what if the police think I had something to do with it?" Cognac asked.

"Why would they think that?" Benita asked.

"Maybe, because it happened last night, and it's already the next day." Regina said.

"So what. And?" Peaches replied.

"If I call them they are going to want to know how I knew what happened. Then there are going to ask me why am I just now saying something. Then they are going to want to know what was I doing there and how did I get in there in the first place. And the fact is I was trespassing, and then they would want to know why was I trespassing. Then they might think I had something to do with it." Cognac expressed.

"Damn, you've got a point." Benita replied.

"So what now?" Peaches asked.

"So what now is I'm going to keep my mouth shut. I don't want anything to do with it... He shouldn't have raped Candace anyway." Cognac replied with a slight mean look on her face.

"Look, maybe you should just relax for a couple of weeks. Take you a breather, and maybe stay with Devin till you get your thoughts together." Regina said, trying to rationalize the whole situation.

"Hmm...I don't know." Cognac replied.

"Or you can stay with me." Regina said.

Cognac looked at Regina, smiled and said "Thanks. What would I do without you?"

"Lose your damn mind?" Regina replied playfully, trying to ease the moment.

"You are a mess." Cognac replied with a smile.

"I'll cook us some grilled chicken and macaroni tonight." Regina said.

"Ok, now you're talking my language." Cognac replied.

"Yeah, mines to! What time is dinner? Me and Peaches gone be there. It will take everybody's minds away from this madness." Benita said very animated.

"Well I guess we just gone have a waiting to exhale party then. Party starts at eight p.m." Regina said happily.

Later that evening will be remarkable over Regina's. Herbed chicken breast grilled to perfection, macaroni baked very cheesy with that perfect crust around the edges and on top.

SORRY

6:05p.m. Cognac had just left Regina's house and had come home to grab a few things. Devin was driving up the street as she stepped inside the house. He pulled up and parked in front of the house. He got out with a beautiful assortment of flowers. He wanted to make up for his inconsideration. He walked up on the porch and rung the doorbell. Cognac was in her bedroom and wondered who it was. She curiously walked back up front to see who it was. She glanced out the window on her way to the door and saw Devin's car in front of the house. She opened up the door and was delighted to see Devin standing there with flowers. She slightly smiled as she opened the door and he stepped in. He gave her a big hug and a kiss on the cheek.

"Ewww you are cold." Cognac said as he wrapped the cold ass arms of his coat around her.

"Sorry baby. These are for you." Devin said as he handed her the flowers and took off his coat.

"Thank you, Ima put them in some water." Cognac said.

"Okay." Devin replied as he took off his coat.

Cognac went and grabbed her crystal vase out of the hallway closet. She went into the kitchen and put some water in it. She put the flowers in it and brought it back out and sat them on the dinning-room table.

"Sweetie..." Devin called out.

"Yes?" Cognac replied.

Devin walked up to her and sincerely looked her in her eyes and said. "Baby, I'm sorry for being inconsiderate. I apologize for accusing you of seeing somebody else especially at a time when you are clearly going through something."

"You okay babe. I know you didn't mean it like that." Cognac said with a slight smile.

"I know, but still. I felt terrible and couldn't wait to get over here and make it right. I let my flawed thoughts get the best of me. I don't like that because you're my flower and I don't ever want to hurt you. I always want to be considerate and understanding of your emotions and feelings." Devin said, as he held her hands caringly.

"And you do, that's why I appreciate you. I don't have to hold a grudge at you when I truly know in my heart that that wasn't your intent." Cognac replied.

"That's what makes me feel like I can do anything in this world for you. I love that you don't see things one sided. You actually understand me too." Devin impressed.

"Of course, that's how it's supposed to be." Cognac replied.

"Well what you got going on today?" Devin asked.

"Well I'm going to hanging over Gina's for a few days."

"Oh okay. Having a little family bonding, that's always good." Devin said, resisting to ask her what's really going on.

Cognac knew deep down inside that he or anyone would be curious about what was going on. She gently put her hands on his arms, took a deep breath and exhaled. She sincerely looked him in his eyes and said. "Honestly, I wish it was just because of family bonding, but it's not... I'm going over to Gina's because...I saw something I wish I never saw.

I swear to you this has nothing to do with me seeing another man, I promise you."

"Well, whatever it is I aint gone let nobody do nothing to you. But, is...somebody after you, or what? I don't even know what I'm protecting you from."

"Really, I don't know...I...I just want to forget about it right now. I want to grab my clothes and a few things and leave. I promise I'll tell you everything later, okay? Don't be mad." Cognac expressed deeply.

Devin pulled her close, hugged her and gently laid her head on his chest. "Baby, I got you, enough said."

The Party! Cognac remembered to ask him about. "Damn, with all of this stuff going on I forgot to ask you if you were okay with just you and Regina running everything tomorrow at the party? I'm not in the right mind state to do it." Sincerely looking up at him.

"Absolutely Baby, you don't have to worry about a thing. I'm on top of things; she's a very smart business woman. I know things will go fine. Plus, I'll be making sure my baby is okay every step of the way." He assured.

Cognac smiled, hugged him tight and said "I love you."

Devin kissed her on the forehead and said "Baby, I love you too." They held each other deeply and close, feeling... each other's heartbeat.

AFTER THOUGHTS

Later that night Angela sat in her kitchen watching the 10 o'clock news. She hadn't heard from Phillip all day. She called him a few times and wondered why he wouldn't answer. There was nothing but bad news being reported about Detroit...as if there were no good things going on in the community. Angela's eyes lit up when she listen to the news caster. Phillip and Edward's faces had flashed on the screen. It was reported that the police had pulled them over about four-thirty in the morning. They found Marcello's body decapitated inside of bags in the trunk of the vehicle. Angela's mouth dropped wide open as her heart pounded. Immediately she was startled as she heard the fearsome screams of her daughter saying "GET OFF OF MEEEEE!!!!!!" Angela darted to her daughter's room and bust the door open. She saw Marcena sitting up in her bed crying and breathing heavily. Angela walked over and sat on the side of Marcena. She hugged her and placed

Marcena's head on her shoulder. Angela started crying as they rocked back and forth.

"It's gonna be okay, sweetie; it was just a nightmare. I swear he will never lay another finger on you." Angela assured with tears streaming down her face.

Marcena cried on Angela's shoulder so innocent and helpless. Angela sat there till she calmed herself a little and laid back down. Angela gently rubbed Marcena's back while gritting her teeth with anger and tears streaming down her face. She wondered how he could put his hands on her. HOW COULD HE DO SUCH A THING TO HER!!! The thought of his bitch ass burning in hell wasn't enough to appease the rage she felt. She could feel Marcena's body slightly quivering nervously. Eventually Marcena calmed down and dozed off. Angela gently got up and went back into the kitchen. Her soul reeked of hate. She walked over to the counter and grabbed a shot glass out of the cabinet. She grabbed a bottle of liquor that was sitting on the counter. She took the cap off, poured her a shot and downed it. It felt like she drank a cup of fire as her throat burned. A wicked scowl was on her face as she pondered thoughts of anger. She started talking to herself as she poured multiple shots and drank them. She grabbed a torn piece of paper and a ink pen that was on the table, leaned over and started writing her thoughts. She was to hyper to sit and frequently nibbled the bottom side of her fingertips.

"I can't believe...he put his hands on her." She uttered to herself with a face full of tears.

"I'm glad his bitch as is dead." She said in a low angered tone.

She poured another shot and said "I wished they would've burned his ass alive."

She looked inside of her glass; her wicked reflection rippled as she shook the table.

"If he would've never messed around with that bitch." She murmured through tightly shut teeth.

"He would've never went to jail and lost his mind. He would've never got out and put his punk ass hands on her... It's her fault...Yeah; it's that bitches fault just as much as it is his. DAMN, DAMN, DAMN!!!" She said to herself furiously as she pounded the table a few times with the side of her fist. She sat down in her kitchen chair and thought about the last time she and Marcello had sex.

She laid on her back with her legs open. She emotionlessly stared at the ceiling while Marcello was on top fucking her. His mind was somewhere else and the sex felt like two people just trying to get each other off. The passion and pleasure of love making was absent. She knew his mind was elsewhere with every lifeless pound. She questioned herself why was she lying here having sex with this nigga. The sweat from his face dripped on hers and had become very irritating. She knew inside that he was fucking around on her. And if he wasn't having sex with someone then he was definitely doing what he wasn't supposed to with whoever the bitch was. She remembered making him get up off of her. Marcello looked at her strange as he got up and stood there.

"So how long you been fucking her?" Angela recalled asking him.

"What the fuck are you talking about?" Marcello replied with an incredulous look on his face.

"You know what the fuck I'm talking about! As of now I'm still your wife regardless of us more than likely going through a divorce!" Angela yelled.

"Where in the fuck are you getting this from?" Marcello asked all while feeling guilty inside and not saying it.

"Marcello, I swear if you gave any type of disease or anything to me Ima kill you." Angela impressed.

"Look, don't come on me with that crazy shit." Marcello replied with guilt written in cursive on his face.

Marcello's cell phone rang; it was on the nightstand by the bed. They both looked at it and saw the name...Cognac. Angela looked right at his ass as he picked his phone up and silenced it.

"Answer the phone, Marcello." Angela said as her heart pounded.

"Why would I answer the phone while we having sex?" Marcello said, irrationally responded, just trying to say anything.

"We aint having a muthafucking thing; we just standing here. Who the fuck is Cognac?" Angela asked as her soul reeked that of violence and rage.

"What you mean who is Cognac?" Marcello asked with his heart pounding and feeling caught up.

"STOP FUCKING PLAYING ME LIKE I'M STUPID!!! Oh, I know...that's that bitch that was on that hair salon flyer that was in your pants pocket." Angela said as she just looked at him.

"Aint nobody playing you like you stupid. And what you doing going through my pockets?" Marcello asked as he grabbed his underwear and put them on.

"I was taking your clothes to the cleaners like you asked me to. But that aint got shit to do with anything so don't get off the subject!" Angela said strongly as a vein surfaced in her neck.

"Look, you tripping. I need to get some air, I'm about to go." Marcello said as he put on his pants and shirt.

"Whatever nigga, you just want to go call that bitch! Get the fuck out!" Angela yelled!

"Aint nobody finna call nobody! Now, I'll talk to you when I get back." Marcello said firmly, putting his foot down and left the room.

"NO, don't come back!" Angela yelled, grabbing a glass off of the dresser and throwing it at him.

Angela remembered the glass hitting the wall and shattering onto the floor. Since Marcello was dead the only one left to blame was Cognac. She sat there trying to remember what Cognac looked like. She thought long and hard as she played back the night she looked at the flyer. Then for some strange reason it dawned on her... That was the same chick she saw in the store. She remembered complimenting Cognac's hat and her saying she has a lot of them. She remembered looking at her I.D. and holding on to it. Immediately she started looking around, she grabbed her purse, searching through it! What the fuck did I do with that damn I.D! It has to be in here... She couldn't find it and stood there for a second with a puzzled look on her face. Damn, what the hell did I do with it? ...Oh well fuck it...might not even be her anyway...or is it? Then she took a deep breath...it couldn't be... That was the same person she saw in the car that morning she pulled up in the alley when they killed Marcello. That would explain who fucking hat that was in the basement of the bar. That also explains why Cognac was rushing like that when she got in the car and pulled the fuck off, and why they found the door open and had no clue who did it. Angela swiftly poured more liquor; damn near a third of a glass. She took a fierce swig, and slammed her glass down on the table splashing liquor on her note. She shook her head, scoffed as her scattered thoughts started coming together, and started making sense. She chuckled and said "You muthafucka... You...mutha...fucka."

NEXT DAY AT THE SALON

February 22, 2012. It was another day another dollar at Essential Beauty Salon. It was about four p.m. and business was going just fine. Neither Regina nor Cognac was there due to family matters. Everyone was doing their usual. Antonio was giving this fine ass woman a pedicure. De 'Juan was doing a lady's hair super sharp; she was going to be in a hair show. Peaches and Benita were working side by side doing their clients hair.

"You heard anything from Regina or Cognac this morning? Peaches asked.

"Regina called me this morning when I opened up, but that was only for a brief second." Benita replied.

"I hope they be okay. They have been going through it." Peaches said.

"Yeah, I know especially Coney. It's been like nonstop drama since 2011 she's been going through it with this guy and then that guy; no type of easy going peaceful relationship. Hell, she need to meet her one of these old ass men that work at Chrysler or something. Somebody that works a hard honest job and too old to be in the street hustling and getting shot at." Benita said.

"Yo behind is ignant. Not ignorant but ignant. But even though you make it sound funny, you're right." Peaches replied.

"Hey well, it might sound funny but I am serious. It's time out for all of that dumb stuff. I'm trying to live, grow old and then pass on. All of these little fast money hustlers I aint got time for. They're just a fast track to problems and an early grave." Benita replied.

"Aye look, speaking of early grave. Did you hear about that fool that died the other day after falling off a building doing that planking?" Peaches asked.

"Again? We were talking about this same mess months ago when a whole bunch of fools were doing that dumb stuff all around town." Benita answered.

"Yes, it happened again. It happened right out there in Farmington Hills yesterday. A lady was on the news saying that she had just got home from work. She walked in and saw her boyfriend and his buddy planking on the balcony of their high rise apartment. She said she told him to get down and stop playing like that. Next thing you know he tried to get down and fell the other way." Peaches said as she was doing a sharp ass hair-do on her client.

"That don't make no damn sense. It's icy as hell outside and you wanna lie on a slippery ass balcony? Hell, I don't want to lay on a row of crates in a house let alone a high ass slippery balcony. People are just flat out dumb, D.U.M.B." Benita spelled out, shaking her head pitifully while tapering the back of her client's neck.

"I know, people are crazy out here." Peaches replied.

I know what it is; these are the days of the crack babies. All the crack babies from back in the day didn't die off when they were little or in their momma's womb. Their behinds grew up into advanced 2012 crack babies." Benita said hilariously.

"Your butt is silly." Peaches said as she laughed.

"Hey, I'm so serious." Benita replied.

"Aye, I know it's been a lot of stuff going on, but are you still going to the party?" Peaches asked.

"Oh yes, I'm ready to get out and party. I hardly hang out at all so I aint bout to miss this." Benita replied.

Just outside a car pulled up out front and parked. The lady inside looked at herself in the mirror and then opened the glove box. Reached in, pulled out a pistol and cocked it. She placed it inside of her purse, and looked at the Essential Beauty Salon flyer she had on the passenger seat. She got out and walked inside. Benita respectably paused her conversation with Peaches to greet the lady as she walked up.

"Hello how are you doing today? How can we help you?" Benita asked.

"Yes, is Cognac in?" The lady asked politely.

"No, she won't be in today. Is there anything I can do for you?" Benita asked with a smile.

"Oh nall, that's okay. Thank you anyway." The lady said as she turned to walk out.

"Who should I say is looking for her?" Benita asked.

The lady replied "...Nook-Nook." And kept walking out.

As she walked out Benita looked at Peaches and said "Damn, she look like she could be Cognac's sister."

"Shit, I thought she was Cognac when she first got out the car." Peaches replied.

"Well you know what they say; we all got a look alike somewhere." Benita said.

Drink & Mingle
@ Status Quo

STATUS QUO

11:01p.m. Status Quo night club was on point. Both floors were banging and people were wall to wall partying. The ambience was sexy and very classy; rich dark colored walls with a wood grain finish. The carpeting was burgundy with a fantastic design. Two huge crystal chandeliers providing the perfect lighting affect. The DJ's on both floors were at the top of their game and playing the hottest tracks. One things fa sho, black folks look good when their out on the dance floor steppin. Everywhere you looked people were enjoying themselves, mixing and mingling. The kitchen staff was ran by Benita and a few family members willing to thoroughly help out. They kept the food fresh and piping hot; five wings and fries for five dollars. Devin stood next to the downstairs bar admiring everything just as Antonio walked up.

"What's happening bro, how you feeling?" Antonio asked as he gave Devin a handshake and hug.

"Chillin, chillin my man. Just enjoying how everything is going. How about you?"

"I'm good man, I'm definitely glad I came."

"I'm glad you came out to. Where's your twin at, is she enjoying herself? I aint been upstairs in a minute."

"Oh, she's enjoying herself. Last time I was upstairs she was talking to Regina and helping her out with whatever."

"Cool, that's wsup...Aye, I got a question if it aint getting to nosey."

"Go ahead, shoot it."

"Are you and Peaches actually a couple or are y'all just dating?"

Antonio was slightly curious of why he asked but wasn't sweating it. "Man, I guess you can say we are; I mean we act like it. However, twice I've told her that I wanted her to be my woman and she'll say in due time, she just doesn't want to rush it. One too many bad choices and broken hearts. Now she runs like a track star when love and commitment comes her way."

"Yeah, that's something else, bro. Can't be letting ole baggage destroy your future. Does she mind if you were dating someone else?"

"That's the thing, hell yeah she minds. She blows up at the thought of another woman trying to get at me or if she thinks I take interest in another woman."

Maybe that's what it's going to take to get her to see that she's got something good and she gone let it slip away."

"I know... and I meet so many beautiful, fine ass women. Doctors, lawyers, all kinds of women and I basically turn they asses down. I done got a few women's numbers here and there and may talk to them from time to time, but it never goes anywhere because I never sincerely give them my energy and time. It just turns out to be a waste of my time and theirs. Why? Because my heart really wants Peaches. I must admit I've lately been starting to think I might need to set my sites elsewhere."

"Ohhhh I've definitely been there before. I dated a woman for three and a half years waiting on her to be ready. Her emotions were always on psycho mode; just irrationally explosive. She was never ever never willing to listen to reason. Whenever we would talk about a problem it was okay for her to ask a question and I respectfully listen, but EVERYTIME I asked her a question that pointed out something she knew she did wrong she would childishly and irrationally say shit that had nothing to do with the situation or idiotically scream or yell to avoid answering the question. It turned out to be a big waste of time. It was a sad ending but now I'm glad it ended... I would've never met Cognac."

"That's wsup bro. How's she doing anyway? Is she still taking things hard?"

"A little bit. She's getting better, but it takes time especially when losing someone so close."

"You're very supportive of her. And out of the few dudes I've Known her to date you're definitely the best person she's had hands down."

"Thanks bro." Devin said as they toasted.

A curious look was on Devin's face as he looked at the entrance. What the hell, I thought she wasn't coming. I'm glad she's here. Cognac walked through the door looking super sexy. She was talking to the lady at the door taking the money, asking how she was doing, and how things were going. A group of Devin's boys were sitting at a couple of tables next to each other having some drinks and jaw jacking. One of them noticed Cognac walk in and their whole conversation immediately stopped!...Damn, who the fuck is that?! Look at them thighs and legs. Look at that ass! Oh, I'm definitely bout ta holla at that. The fellas were going crazy; gawking at her, trying to play it off. Cognac saw Devin to her left over at the bar as soon as she stepped in the club. She walked through the reservoir double doors looking like a celebrity. Naturally her hips swayed from left to right. She wore her hair in a jazzy fly Mohawk that many women envied and admired. Her short fur coat was exquisite, and her body fitting leoprod dress amplifide her dynamic figure extremely causing all that looked at her to have a brief moment of fuckin silence. As soon as she was walking pass the fellas she heard one guy say "Excuse me sexy, can I talk to you for a minute?"

Cognac politely smiled and said "I can't, my man right here, boo." Pointing at Devin as she kept walking.

Their eyes were glued to her body every step of the way till she approached the bar. That's when they saw Devin smiling, and saluting them like Yeah niggas, that's right this is all me. You can look but you can't touch. A ménage a trios? Sorry bro's I aint sharing this one...unless it's with another woman! Devin gave Cognac a big loving hug just as she approached him.

"You gotta excuse my boy's babe; they can be hounds some times." Devin said.

"No problem bay, I aint thinking about them."

"That's why you my boo, baby. I'm glad you came." Devin said to her with a smile.

"Thank you, baby. I'm glad I came to. I just decided I didn't want to keep being stuck in the house; it wouldn't change anything." Cognac replied.

"That's true. Well, you want something to drink, a glass of Mascoto maybe?"

"Yes, but first I want to go holla at Regina and see how she's doing and then chill if that's cool?"

"Of course it's cool; let's go upstairs, that's where they're at." Devin suggested.

Cognac looked over at Antonio. "Hey A."

"Wdup Coney, you okay?" Antonio asked, sincerely.

"Yeah, I'm okay. Aint no need in sitting around constantly sulking in misery. So I came to enjoy myself; that's what auntie would want me to do anyway." Cognac smiled.

"I know that's right."

"Well, I'ma go holla at Gina for a second, and then I'm ready to party."

"Okay."

Before they walked upstairs Devin turned around and said to Antonio. "Just remember, often we place current relationships on hold to find that which looks better. But that which looks better never promises true love. And by the next time you possibly find true love those looks may be long gone."

Devin turned and walked away with Cognac. Devin's fellas couldn't wait till Devin and Cognac walked back pass. They tried hard to not to stare while as they approached them, but when they walked pass...them niggas salivated and gawked like hell. Man gaud damn she got a fat ass, dog. I'll beat the brakes off her ass! Them niggas went back to their other conversation once Cognac's ass turned the corner and they walked upstairs and they couldn't see her no more. Antonio stayed by the bar sipping his brew, thinking about what Devin was talking about. That was some real shit. Regina and Peaches were upstairs talking. As soon as they saw Cognac come through the upstairs door they got excited! Coney!!!!!!!!! They happily walked over to her and group hugged her. Cognac loved the loving embrace. They all kicked it about how everything was going; everything was all good. After that it was party time. Devin held it down while the ladies shared a few drinks and then got on the dance floor. Devin went back downstairs and checked on the money at the door. Twenty to thirty minutes later Cognac decided to come back down the stairs. On her way down she was stopped by one of Devin's boys. He was digging the hell out of her and couldn't pass up the opportunity. He grabbed on to the rail so she couldn't proceed pass.

"Excuse me, I need to get pass please." Cognac said.

"Hold on baby, I just want to say something to you." Robert said with his words slurring.

This nigga drunk as fuck and his breath stank. I wish he would get the fuck out my way. He irritating as hell and I'm getting pissed. He knows damn well he wouldn't be up in my face if Devin was around ole disrespectful nigga. "Okay, what is it because I need to go."

"I just wanna say you look sexy as fuck and I wanna holla at you." Robert said, looking at her all drunk with legs slightly staggering.

"Okay, aint Devin your friend?" Cognac looked at him sideways.

"I mean...we cool and shit, but not like that...he aint gotta know." Robert was moving up on her.

"Well, let me tell you that you are being very disrespectful. You're too close, you all up in my face, and as far as him not knowing, I know it so that's just as bad."

"Damn, baby why you trippin? Don't knock it until you've tried it." Robert said, moving up on her trying to kiss her neck.

Get yo drunk ass the fuck off of me! I can't stand no class having stupid ass dudes. Cognac held on to the rail trying to stop herself from falling back on the stairs. With her other arm she was trying to push him up off of her. He was drunk and persistent. His eyes looked sluggish, and his beer breath smelled like straight ass. Her wishes for him to stop went in one ear and out the other. He really went over the line and pulled her to him. Get your fuckin hands off of me you disrespectful bastard! He gripped her waist with one hand and grabbed her ass with the other. She shoved his ass down a couple of stairs and he caught his balance. He didn't give a fuck and he charged back up the stairs. Devin was leading his boys up the stairs and saw what the hell this fool was doing!

"Devin, yo boy is disrespecting me!"

Devin immediately charged up the stairs and grabbed Robert. What the fuck is you doing?! Devin slung Robert down the stairs. He tried to grip the railing and stop his fall; luckily his boys caught him. Robert got pissed and tried to charge at Devin but his boys held his ignorant ass back. Devin regained control; after all he had money invested in this party. He couldn't afford for a big fight to break out and the police shut the party down.

"Somebody get his drunk ass out of here." Devin said.

"How you gone try to play me over a bitch you hoe ass nigga?!" Robert asked, sounding like a straight juvenile heathen.

"Ima show you who the bitch is!" Devin retorted, trying to muscle his way to him. His boys stayed in between them.

"Come on nigga, I'm here. I'm right here, nigga!!" Robert said very animated.

"Dog, you drunk and talking dumb. Get your ass up out of here before I have to beat yo ass." Devin replied with a mean mug on his face.

The fellas were pulling on Robert trying to get him up out of there. They knew he was way the hell out of line. Robert was still talking shit with slurred words. "You aint gone beat shit, nigga! You aint gone beat shit!!"

By that time the bouncers rushed over and made sure Robert got the heck out of there. Devin's boys were completely embarrassed, and pissed that Robert would do that back stabbing shit. One of the fellas went outside and eventually calmed Robert down and took him home. Devin turned around and stepped up the stairs to make sure Cognac was okay.

"Baby, you okay?" Devin asked.

"Yeah I'm cool; I aint trippin." Cognac replied.

Devin rubbed his face, shook his head and blurted out in frustration "Damn, I can't stand ole juvenile niggas that get drunk and fuck shit up! Just loud mouth, ignorant buffoons."

"I know, but don't let it all worked up. We got more important fish to fry tonight."

"I know...you're right. But wait, did he hurt you? How did it happen?" Devin asked as they stepped all the way back up on the landing.

"Naw, he didn't hurt me. He was trying to holla at me, I turned him down, and he wasn't taking no for an answer. He started getting aggressive and trying to put his hands on me. I pushed him down the stairs and when he came back at me is when you ran up and grabbed him." Cognac answered.

"I apologize, baby." Devin said.

"It's cool; I just want to enjoy the party, put some money in our pockets and go home." Cognac, fixed her clothing.

"I'm with that." Devin, fixed his clothes as well.

"And um, momma can use a good back massage later on tonight." Cognac said, glancing at him with a smirk and turned to go back into the party.

"No problem, Daddy gotcha covered baby." Devin replied, smacking her on the ass as they walked back in to enjoy the party.

ESSENTIAL BEAUTY SALON...YOU ALREADY KNOW WHAT TO EXPECT

February 23, 2012, 11:47a.m. Day after the big party it was time to get back on the grind beautifying clients. Everyone was there and feeling fantastic especially after last night. The scent of hair being straightened with hot combs and curled with curling irons was in the air. Ladies were in there getting their hair whipped. It's always a pleasure to see Benita doing someone's locks. If you're looking for that clean, urban, soulful, gorgeous natural look Benita's the lady you wanna see. De'Juan had just walked in not too long ago and was getting ready for his first client. Regina, Peaches and Antonio were doing their normal thing making their clients look top notch. Cognac was back in action. She had just finished up with a client and was wiping down her area getting ready for her next. Benita was amped up from last night and always keeps the conversations coming. Benita looked over at Peaches and asked

"Girl, did you see big boy on the floor getting down last night?

"I shole the hell did. The way he was moving out there, doing them splits I just knew he was going to bust a hole in his slacks!" Peaches replied, laughing.

Cognac burst out laughing and chimed in "I swear to goodness I took my phone out and put it on camcorder. I recorded the hell out of that man. If he would've slipped and fell, or bust his pants off by doing all them damn splits like he was James Brown I swear I was going to be YouTubing that!"

"Are you serious, you recorded him?" Benita asked.

"Heck yeah she did with her silly self; had me over there cracking up the whole time. She kept saying he's finna fall and bust his ass any second now! You think it was wrong for her to record him?" Regina asked Benita.

"Hell nall, I wanna see it. I feel like laughing my ass off again! I aint never laughed that hard; my stomach was hurting from laughing so much I almost curled up like a fetus!" Benita replied.

"You are a damn fool, you know that?" Peaches said, laughing.

"Whatever, I'm serious. I aint never seen a big fella move like that before. He had to be about 5'7' and every bit of three hundred pounds. It was like watching a big bowl of jello shaking in a wild earthquake!" Benita replied very silly and animate.

"Hey, but you gotta admit he was killing them other folks out there on that floor. He was on point with every beat. They needed to take lessons from him." Regina added.

They all looked as the front door opened. Everyone was all smiles once they realized it was Mrs. Sarah Langston walking through the door. She was about to have Regina do her hair. Even some of the clients recognized her, smiled and spoke to her as well. She took her coat off and hung it on the coat rack; the staff took turns giving her welcome hugs. Sarah was delighted to see how well kept and professional they were running the place. Sarah walked up and Cognac gave her a big hug and smile. Sarah was like an aunt or a God Mother to her and Regina. She always had something positive to say.

"Girl you're always looking good and fantastic." Sarah said, with a pleasant smile.

"Thank you so much; you know you always make my day. It don't matter if it's in person or over the phone." Cognac replied.

"How have you been?" Sarah asked.

"I've been okay; I mean...outside of the drama I have been through this past year and a half I'm still good." Cognac replied.

"That's good, how is little Eric?" Sarah asked.

"He's fine, and he's been doing good in school." Cognac replied.

"That is so good. I am so proud of you." Sarah so proudly said with a smile.

"Thank you, your words mean a lot to me." Cognac replied.

Sarah looked over at Regina and took a deep breath. "And this woman right here, I'm so proud of her too. I love how you have been doing things around here. I'm proud of the whole staff because you couldn't have done it without them."

"Of course not, I love them; this is the fam right here." Regina replied as she was finishing up her client.

"How are you and Mr. Marlon doing?" Sarah asked.

"Um...were sort of off and on. I don't think it's going to work though."

"Oh no? I'm sorry to hear that. I thought you guys were doing just fine."

"Yeah we were, but... it just seemed that he always had a problem with me making more money that him. It was like a power thing with him. He seem like he would go out of his way to be in control or let me know that he was the man."

"Oh, that's not good." Sarah replied.

"Hell nall it aint good; aint no man controlling me. I make the money, I call the shots." Peaches client, Karen butted in and replied.

"Yeah, I can't have no man that's over controlling. I don't mind being submissive to my man. But controlled? Hecks no." Benita said, glancing at Regina.

"Submissive? That's just another way of being controlled; to hell with that. All men want to do is control you, tell you what to do, tell you to give them sex whenever THEY want it etc, etc." Karen replied.

Antonio hated sexist comments. He looked over at her and asked "Excuse me, if you don't mind me asking, do you have a man?"

Karen looked at him for a second answered "No."

Men-Tal

Antonio just nodded his head while he continued working on his client and thinking. *That's exactly what I thought. Of course you don't have a man. Aint no man gone want to put up with all of that stank attitude and you gone forever be lonely.*

Karen wanted to know what was all of that head nodding for. *What the fuck you trying to say?* She waited for a second and asked "So what you trying to say?"

Antonio calmly looked at her and answered. "I didn't say anything."

"You didn't have to say anything." Karen responded.

"Karen, calm down. It's going to be alright." Peaches, not liking how she seemed edgy with Antonio.

"Okay look...maybe if you didn't have a nasty attitude a man wouldn't have a reason to try and control you. Which leads me to my question for you. Is it that you don't want a controlling man or...is it that you don't want a man stopping you from acting out of control, especially with your attitude? You have to learn to be easy and communicate right." Antonio replied.

"I don't have an attitude, and I communicate right enough." Karen replied.

Can't see ya flaws, don't want to see ya flaws. You're just going to be a miserable lonely old bag with an attitude. Antonio kept his thoughts to his self. He knew that anything he said she would twist it and he didn't feel like hearing no more of her mouth or attitude.

Sarah saw a reason for her to interrupt. Karen butted into a conversation that had nothing to do with her and used it to vent.

"Hey, beautiful people, beautiful people; there's no need to bicker. And yes, we do have to learn to communicate right; it's the only way we can thoroughly understand a problem in order to address it properly." Sarah said, respectfully.

"Yeah, you're right." Karen calmed down and replied.

"Mrs. Langston, before we drift away from the story. Why do you think relationships have so many problems when the woman is the bread winner?" Benita asked.

"Well, when you're on subject such as this you have to have a very open mind. There are plenty of different scenarios, because you have millions of different people with millions of different personalities.

However, submission and control doesn't have to have anything to do with the other. Submission is something that is supposed to be respectfully rendered along with the love and honor you have for your mate. There's nothing wrong with a woman being submissive to her husband. And no husband should abuse that privilege and maliciously dominate his wife. The part that people don't see is that men are submissive to their mates and wives as well. Men give into women all of the time just as women give into their men. We just have to learn not to abuse the privilege and the one we love." Sarah said.

"Okay then, what is control to you?" Karen asked.

"When you talk about control you have to realize that money gives you control in many cases. The problem is a lot of people don't know how to have money, still be who they were before they got it and not let the power control them. Think about it, the people that control what's going on are the people that have the money. Money will always be affiliated with power and control whether we like it or not. This gives birth to the old cliché you make the money and never let the money make you." Sarah preached.

"I know that's right!" Cognac concurred.

"Can I say something?" Antonio respectfully asked.

Sarah looked at him with a smile and said. "Please do."

"There's nothing wrong with a woman making more money than a man; that's just more money for the household. I think in many cases the problem is that some women...not all, but some...tend to look down on their men because they make more money. It's like dishonor and disrespect comes along with it. Whereas if the man makes the most money she's more humble." Antonio expressed.

"I've dealt with many cases like that where the bread winner of the couple tends to lose respect and honor for their mate be it the man or the woman. However, just because you make the most money and it renders you a sense of control does not mean you're not supposed to control yourself." Sarah replied.

"Hey, like the Goddess said, you make the money and don't let the money make you." Cognac replied.

It was time for Sarah to sit down so she could get her hair done. But before she did she turned to Cognac and said to her personally while everybody started talking about something else. "It was put on my heart to say this to you. You have a beautiful bright future ahead of you. I know you've been through so much this last year or so. There's always sunshine after the rain. And even after that more rain will come; it just goes hand and hand. But you're a warrior, so when it comes just make sure you stay resilient, and endure. The most high is protecting you...for a reason."

Cognac took that to heart without a smile. Damn, that was deep.

YES, RIGHT THERE

February 23, 2012, 9:17p.m. Cognac and Devin laid in a spooning position in Cognac's comfy king size bed. Her eyes closed peacefully as she leaned her head forward. Devin's hands firmly gripped her shoulders as his thumbs massaged her back and neck. It felt like a euphoric paradise as his thumbs stiffly pressed over the built up tension. He leaned forward gently placing wet kisses on the back of her neck. He slid his left hand around sensually feeling on her breast. She loved every bit of it as her pussy got extremely wet. His dick felt like a hard cucumber pressed up against her ass. He lightly nibbled her ear as he slid his hand down in between her thighs. Down in her panties his middle finger fiddled with her pussy lips. Sensually nibbling, lightly biting her shoulders and neck he started finger fucking her. After a brief moment he needed to satisfy his crave. His tongue salivated for the taste of her pussy. It was an unexplainable turn on whenever she put her ass in his face or rode his mouth. He got up and had her lie on her back. He carefully pulled her to the edge of the bed and parted her legs. He kissed her right ankle, and then her calf. He lightly kissed the back of her knee tracing his tongue down the middle of her thigh. The sensation gave her the ultimate rush, and vaginal stimulation. Her pulse and breathing accelerated. And then...and then... he traced his wet tongue all the way down her thigh...and then...he passionately French kissed the fuck out of her pussy. "OH MY GAUD, this feel so fucking good!!!" Cognac yelled as she gripped the back of his head. He sucked her clitoris swallowing the sweet nectar of her peach. He knew she was cummin as her body tensed and quivered. She breathed harder as her fingernails gripped his scalp!! She moaned and fucking moaned as she felt that shit about to explode. FUCK, FUCK!!!!...she came hard as a muthafucka!! Cum saturated his goatee as he enjoyed watching her reaction. Watching how her body quivered, and how firmly her toes curled. He stood straight up and stuck his stiff ass dick all in her pussy. He wrapped her legs around his neck and fucked the shit out of her on the side of the bed. Every stroke felt like a euphoric thunder. She moaned and made every type of freak nasty fuck face you could imagine. He did it till she could hardly handle anymore. "Oh fuck!" she yelled as she creamed all over his dick. He started hitting it faster, and faster, she knew he was about to blast off!! He tapped that ass, and stroked and fucked till he couldn't hold back any longer. He pulled his dick out and she immediately got down on her knees. He jacked his dick, making it cum all on her thick lips. She put his dick in her mouth and sucked, and sucked until he had to actually pull back from her because he couldn't take no more. He had to stand back and catch his damn breath. Unexpectedly the doorbell rang.

"I wonder who that is...Oh it's probably Eric bringing little Eric home." Cognac said.

"Oh okay." Devin said as he got his cloths and walked into the bathroom.

Cognac quickly put her clothes back on and rushed to the door. She heard women's voices at the door and remembered the girls were coming over. She looked outside and opened the door. It was Regina, Peaches, and Benita. She unlocked the screen door and let them in.

"Wdup girl?" Regina asked as she took off her coat and shoes at the door.

"Nothing much, just bout to freshen up real quick. Y'all already know make y'all self at home. I'll be right back out here." Cognac said as she walked into the bedroom.

Cognac grabbed her some panties, bra, pants and shirt. She went into the bathroom with Devin and hoped in the shower with him. They quickly washed each other up and got out. They dried off and put on their cloths. They walked out and joined the rest of everybody. Cognac looked outside and saw her son's father's car pull up in the driveway. The passenger door opened and little Eric got out. Cognac walked to the door and opened it as Eric ran up on the porch. She waved at Big Eric as he pulled out of the driveway and pulled off. Cognac hugged and kissed her son as he stepped inside and shut the door. He took off his boots and left them in the middle of the floor. He did responsibly hang his coat up in the closet and went in living-room and spoke.

"Um...Eric." Cognac said with an eyebrow raised and her hand on her hip.

"Huh ma?" Eric answered as he turned around.

"Where do your boots belong?" Cognac asked.

"Oh....in the corner." Eric replied.

"Okay, chop chop." Cognac said, implying for him to hurry up and move his shoes.

"Sorry mom." Eric said very high spirited as he went and put his boots in the corner.

All the grown folks had decided they wanted to go to the store and get some liquor to drink. Eric quickly walked over to Devin and asked if he wanted to play basketball on the Xbox with him. Devin told him to go set it up and he'll be in there in a moment to play with him. Eric ran in the room to get it going. All the ladies had decided that they would run to the store together. Devin could stay at the house and play the game with Eric. Devin said that he would sponsor the drinks. He pulled a fifty dollar bill out of his pocket and handed it to Cognac. He went in the room to play the game with Eric. The ladies put on their wraps and went out to find a liquor store that wasn't closed.

Men-Tal

UNEXPECTED GUEST

Angela drove west going up Seven Mile Rd. A large brown box with something in it sat on the passenger seat. Multiple thoughts of ill shit that happened in her life went through her mind. Scared by her past she never found what it took to forgive and let go. Her daily smile was mostly a façade to mask the hate within. What happened to her daughter was the last straw. EVERYBODY IS MARKED FOR DEATH NOW!!! She looked at the street signs searching for the right block but none had rung a bell. She breathed deeply and thought hard as she could to recall the address. She remembered the store clerk handing her the I.D. She remembered looking at Cognac's face, and thinking she was nice looking but didn't have shit on her. However, the address for some reason was vague in her mind, but she couldn't remember it. Damn, what the fuck is that bitches address?!! I can't believe I lost that fuckin I.D! Ha Ha; Oooooooohhhhhh yes bitch you can't stop me; I'm going to find yo ass. She got a bright idea and pulled up in a gas station and parked. She grabbed her cell phone, unlocked it and went on the internet. She looked up White Page phone book and accessed the site. She smirked as she thought how easy it is to find somebody you're looking for. Right where it ask for the person's name she typed in the name she saw on Cognac's I.D. Behold the site provided her full name, age, city, state and country she lived in, but didn't provide the exact address unless signed up and paid for full access to the site. FUCK!!...I know this is this bitch...Hmmm, I wonder if this gas station has a White Pages phonebook I can use real quick? She put her phone in her holster and got out of the car. A base-head was standing by the entrance looking absolutely un-kept and nasty as fuck. His nappy ass unshaved face, and extremely ashy chapped lips made it look like his breath smell like hot, wet elephant shit. Politely as he could he asked her Mam, can I pump your gas for you or can you spare a little change? Angela didn't want to be bothered with at the time and replied with a seriously fierce look on her face Please don't fuck with me right now, sir. She walked into the gas station and stood behind the person at the counter.

Impatiently she looked up at the ceiling while tapping her fingertips on the counter wishing this slow muthafucka in front of her will hurry up and make up their mind about what the fuck they were going to buy and get the fuck on so she could go. Finally, you slow bitch! She gave an ill nasty look as the customer walked out the door. She stepped up and asked the clerk "Do you have a White Pages I can borrow for a second?" Not really wanting to help her out he replied "No, I'm sorry we don't have White Pages here." Angela turned and headed out the gas station but she abruptly stopped as the attendant had a change of heart and got her attention. He felt wrong for being that way and said "Ms. I'm sorry but we have White Pages right here; you can use it. I must've looked over it somehow." Angela turned around and stepped to the counter thinking Bitch, you knew you had it the whole time; you should've said that shit in the first place. He slid her the White Pages and she replied Thank you. She carried it over to the side; not because she was being courteous to others so they could pay for their stuff; she just didn't want everybody else all up in her business. She swiftly flipped through the pages and eventually found a match with the name and information in her phone. She grabbed the ink pen that was lying on the counter. She noticed a no good lottery ticket on the floor, picked it up and wrote the address down on the back of it. Her pulse accelerated as she left the White Pages right there and quickly walked the fuck out. The attendant looked at her like Aye you aint gone give me my fuckin White Pages back bitch, but she didn't give a fuck. She could taste revenge on the tip of her tongue like a dab of potent cocaine; she was ready! She hopped in her ride, started it up and peeled swiftly out of the gas station. She checked her rearview as she drove up the road; didn't want to get stopped by the police. Wicked thoughts induced a nasty snarl on her face as she road through the night in search for Cognac's street. Here this muthafuckin street is! Say hello to the bad guy, bitches! Finally she arrived at the street and made a right turn. Thoroughly she peered at each address on the houses. She eased pass house after house after house and then...Bingo, it's show time. She slowed up and then pulled over and parked. She looked back at the house; wondering if anyone was looking out the window or something. She got out of the car with the box and shut the door behind her. She vigilantly looked around as she approached the house. She walked up on the porch and then rung the doorbell. Impatiently she knocked on the door as well. Inside Eric was whooping Devin's butt in the basketball game. Devin paused the game when he heard the doorbell ring. He was thinking damn be patient and give him a second to get to the door. He figured maybe Cognac left her key or something. "I'll be right back young fella, this aint over. You're going down." Devin said as he headed for the front door. There was a knock at the door again. "Here I come." Devin said as he approached the door. He opened the door and was surprised to see this strange woman. He just knew it was going to be Coney and them at the door with the drinks. She was nice looking and didn't seem to pose a threat.

"Hello, you looking for Cognac, I mean Rachelle?" Devin asked.

"Yes, is she here?" Angela asked.

"Naw, she just stepped out, but she will be right back though."

"Are you serious? Man, that girl don't never stay put." Angela said, pretending like she's one of Cognac's good friends.

"I know, right." Devin replied.

"Oh well... Can you give her this, and tell her Angela came bye?"

"Oh yeah, no problem." Devin said as he opened the screen door.

Angela handed him the box and soon as he grabbed it she had the pistol in her right hand. She aimed it at him and told him to back the fuck up. Devin's eyes got big as two boiled eggs and his heart rushed like fuck! Angela stepped in and shut the door behind her. She was dangerously in love with the control and power she possessed with the gun in her hand.

"Don't scream, just do as I say." Angela said, looking at him with a hollow stare.

The cold look in her eyes made him think she would kill him with no remorse. She made him walk into the dinning-room calmly. She had him sit the box on the table. She told him to close the blinds to the dinning-room windows. She said don't get no bright ideas and had him sit down in a chair. They were back against the far wall and facing the living-room. She needed to see

Cognac first when she came in. Angela looked when she heard footsteps and a voice.

"Is that momma?" Eric asked as he walked out of the bedroom.

She surmised it was a young boy from the light tone of his voice. She saw his shadow on the wall from the hallway light. As soon as he turned the corner she said "Come sit right here lil fella." Angela cautiously pulled out a chair along side of Devin. If Devin would've tried to get slick and move an inch she was gone blast the shit out of him and Eric. Eric immediately got scared and wanted to run for freedom and help. Angela aimed the gun at him and said "DO NOT RUN. Come sit your little ass down if you want to see your momma again."

"Please don't shoot him! Eric, come sit down, it's going to be okay." Devin said, trying not to show his nervousness to Eric.

Eric paused for a second with a face full of fear, confusion, and he was breathing hard. He looked at Devin, glanced at Angela and then back at Devin. Devin just wanted Eric to just do as she says so they both don't get killed. "Just come sit down, Eric. She's not going to hurt us." Devin assured, glancing over at Angela unsure about anything he just said. Angela just looked at Devin for a second. Don't getcha hopes up nigga. If I'm going to kill this braud do you really think I'm going to let you two muthafucka's live. That would be stupid as fuckin hell. I should just shoot yo stupid ass right now for saying that stupid shit. Eric hesitantly eased over and sat down. Angela stepped over and stood behind Eric. She placed her left hand on his shoulder and her right hand clutched the pistol. She looked over at Devin with that cold wicked stare.

"Please...he's just a little boy. He aint did nothing to nobody." Devin pleaded, scared for both of their lives.

"Is there anyone else here?" Angela asked.

"No." Devin replied.

"I swear if you lie to me Ima kill you first." Angela promised.

"Mam, you aint even gotta do this. We aint did nothing to nobody." Devin said, pleading for their lives.

Angela put the gun up to her lips and said "Shhhhhh...just comply with the rules and it won't hurt a bit."

Devin calmed himself just a tad bit though his hands showed slight vibration. He prayed and prayed and prayed like a devoted

Men-Tal

Monk with nothing else to do. What the fuck did Cognac do to this bitch he thought to himself? Did she steal something from her ass? Did she fuck this crazy bitch's man? What the fuck is this bitch gone do when Cognac and them finally walk in the house. She was a little bit too far away for him to try and pull off some heroic slick shit and grab her. Instead he opted to be patient and just wait it out. If she got to blasting he was gone try to dive through the nearest window and hope he comes out of this alive. He built up the nerve to ask a question.

"Why are you doing this?" Devin asked.

"Because I have to." Angela replied.

"You have to? Why do you have to do this? We didn't do anything to you." Devin replied.

"Haven't you ever heard of death by association?" Angela asked.

Yeah but...you...you don't have to do this. What about forgiveness? Can't you forgive whatever was done to you?" Devin nervously asked.

Angela wickedly chuckled and replied "Forgiveness? Forgiveness? Sometimes forgiveness comes by way of redemption.

You redeem yourself and then afterwards forgive yourself."

"Can't we just talk about this and we all walk away unharmed?" Devin asked, thinking Cognac and them would be coming through the door soon.

"SHUT THE FUCK UP!!!! I don't want to talk about shit with you!... Your voice is irritating and I'm trying to think. Aint that what y'all men say to us women? Angela asked.

Devin started to humbly answer her and Angela immediately said "I said shut the fuck up now shut the fuck up!!... I'm trying to think here."

They heard car doors closing outside. Cognac and them had finally made it back. She gripped Eric's shoulder very tight! Eric whimpered a little bit and Devin got ready to ask her to please don't hurt him. Angela looked over at Devin and said "Quiet. If you say a word I swear I will kill every last one of y'all. I will take your I.D's, look your names up on the internet and find your families and kill them too. Now please don't piss me off." Cognac unlocked the door and they all stepped in, taking their wraps off.

"Damn, it's quiet." Peaches said.

"I know, they probably back there all into that game. Devin a big ass kid too." Cognac said as she hung up her coat.

Regina walked into the living-room and suddenly stood there in shock. She was petrified with her mouth opened.

"Oh my God..." Regina said, nervously covering her mouth.

Cognac's heart immediately started beating nervously. Peaches and Benita was wondering what the hell could be wrong. They were praying Devin didn't do something bad to Eric or nothing like that. Cognac walked over and looked into the dinning-room. Her face immediately saddened. She felt helpless like her life was hanging halfway over the edge of a steep violent cliff...and she just hadn't been pushed over to her death yet.

"You're...you're the lady from the store." Cognac said, pitifully.

Devin was looking like what the fuck? And then it registered that she was the lady that handed Cognac her I.D.

"Yes...I am." Angela replied.

Peaches and Benita were petrified in disbelief. Could this really be fucking happening?

Angela held the gun over Eric small chest and said "You know what? All of y'all sit the fuck down in here at this table!"

Everyone nervously eased into the dinning-room and carefully sat down.

"No, you stand up." Angela said, looking at Cognac.

The looks upon their faces were bleak. They wondered to themselves is this how it ends? Why is this happening? Benita prayed about seventy-three times that she could just wake up and all of this just be a nightmare.

"You're the lady that came up to the shop. You're Ms. Nook-Nook, right?" Benita asked, nervously.

"Yes, I'm Mrs. Fuckin Nook-Nook, government name Angela. New name Grim Reaper if you keep fuckin talking." Angela replied.

Peaches was shaking and looking even more petrified and spellbound. It didn't dawn on her at first that that's who she was until Benita asked her. Cognac stood there bewildered but calm. She didn't want Angela to shoot her son or anyone else. Cognac took a deep breath and peacefully asked "Why are you doing this?" Angela took a calm breath; slightly chuckled and replied "...I finally have the honor...to meet the woman who fucked up my life. The woman who fucked up my home. The woman who was a part of a young girl's innocence being snatched and soul scared forever. A young innocent girl helplessly raped by her father... If it wasn't for you I would still be married to my husband and he would be here." Angela's face bared more evil than that of a luciferian.

"Mam...with all do respect I haven't wrecked anyone's home. I haven't had anyone raped. Please believe me I don't know what you're talking about." Cognac uttered calmly.

"DON'T FUCKING LIE TO ME!!!!! You know what the fuck I'm talking about!" Angela said as she aimed the gun at her.

Cognac did not want to say the wrong thing and make Angela get to blasting. She uttered extremely nervously "Mam, I swear...this is the only man I've been with over the last six months. Please tell me you aint talking about Devin."

"I aint her man!" Devin said trying to keep his name out of it.

"Didn't I tell you your voice was fucking irritating?" Angela said slow and deeply.

"Please, I'm sorry. You're right, just don't shoot." Devin said, trying not to get the shit shot out of his ass.

Angela looked back at Cognac and said "No, I'm not talking about this scared muthafucka right here. My husband would've still been running his fucking mouth, trying to be tuff and got a bullet in his ass... The part that's killing me is... You're looking at me like you don't know who I'm talking about... Look inside of that box... maybe it will help ring a bell."

Cognac looked at the box strangely. She had no damn clue what was in that box. Was it a bomb, something incriminating. Could it be dead body parts, a live snake or something to jump out on her? She was super fucking nervous about even touching it.

"Stop procrastinating and open the fucking box." Angela said very angrily.

Cognac took a deep breath and fearfully opened the box. Her mouth dropped wide open when she saw what was inside. Oh my fuckin dam, where did she get this from? Damn, that's why I couldn't find my hat; I left it at the bar that night! What could she possibly know? Is she trying to blackmail some money out of me? FUCK! She was the lady in the car that night, pulling pass me. Devin, Benita, and everyone was curious as hell as of what was inside that box. Cognac pitifully looked at Angela and asked "Marcello was your husband?"

"Yes he fucking was...now go ahead, take it out of the box." Angela said wickedly.

Cognac nervously reached inside of the box and grabbed the hat. Her soul felt exposed, hollow and helpless. The fear and pressure made it feel slightly difficult to breath.

"Now put it on." Angela said.

Cognac looked at Angela wondering why she is doing this.

"Put the fucking hat on." Angela said.

Cognac nervously put the hat on, and looked at Angela. Angela sinisterly chuckled again and said "Aw, don't you look nice and pretty... IS THAT HOW YOU LOOKED WHEN YOU STOLE MY FUCKIN HUSBAND AND WRECKED MY FUCKING HOME?!!!!!!!!!!!!!" Angela asked as she pointed the gun directly at Cognac's heart.

Cognac could do nothing but tell her the truth and hope she believed her. Cognac knew that there was nothing she could do.

She was at the mercy of Angela and her pistol.

"I swear... when I met Marcello... he told me he was single. He never wore a ring and never mentioned anything about you, I swear." Cognac innocently pleaded.

Angela looked at her with an angry yet sorrowed face. She felt dire rage, animosity and yelled "LIAR!!! I know you knew!"

Everyone was very scared as Angela became more wroth. The scowl on her face was ruthless. However, Angela slightly felt Cognac was telling the truth, but didn't really want to accept it. Angela felt wrongfully stripped and robbed. Vengeance was on the edge of her finger and she wanted redemption on somebody. EVERYBODY COULD GET IT!! A tear dripped down the side of her face and her lip trembled.

"I swear on my life I never knew..." Cognac calmly pleaded.

At that time Cognac closed her eyes and recalled the precious words of Mrs. Sarah Langston. It was put on my heart to say this to you. You have a beautiful bright future ahead of you. I know you've been through so much this last year or so. There's always sunshine after the rain. And even after that more rain will come; it just goes hand and hand. But you're a warrior, so when it comes just make sure you stay resilient, and endure. The most high is protecting you...for a reason. Cognac opened her eyes and just looked at her. Angela breathed heavily as she stood there ominously looking back at her. Her nostrils flared as she kept the pistol pointed at her. She slowly walked over to Cognac and placed the barrel of the gun on her breast. Angela had a face full of anger and tears. She tried to hold back from crying but couldn't. She looked Cognac directly in her eyes.

"If you would've never come into his life...he would've never gone to jail. THEY SODOMIZED HIM WHILE HE WAS IN THERE!!!!... It drove him crazy...crazy enough that he raped his own daughter. It's your fault!... It's your fault he put his fucking grimy hands on my child... She didn't deserve it...she did nothing to no one... I made him pay though. Lately I had been fucking his boy; I knew he would do whatever I wanted him to do. Anybody that was close to Marcello knew him and Phillip were tight. But not tighter than this pussy and I made him kill that sorry bastard." Angela impressed deeply with her gun trembling in hand.

"...Angela, you know I didn't do it... And blaming me for what he did won't change what happened to your daughter. I hate him to...he raped my younger cousin the night my aunt died...he beat her up as well and hospitalized her. But if you must kill me...just let them go...they had nothing to do with it." Cognac softly expressed.

More tears came streaming down Angela's partially angered, partially saddened face. With the pistol still aimed at Cognac she began to slowly step sideways towards the living-room. Everyone looked on with fear and disbelief. She slowly stepped backwards into the living-room. Angela whimpered and sniffled as she eased backwards towards the front door. With her eye and steady aim on Cognac she reached behind her and opened the door. She lowered the gun and they stood there looking at each other. Angela felt hurt and cheated with no one to blame it on. Cognac looked at her with more sympathy than fear. Angela eased on out the door and headed for the car. Eric immediately ran over and hugged Cognac. Devin and everyone else got up and hugged her as well. And with all the embrace Cognac was blown away by everything that had been taking place in her life. She decided she needed to get away. Away from all these crazy situations, headaches and drama. Just away and enjoy a piece of life.

If A Picture
Is Worth
A Thousand Words...
Then This
Facial Expression
Is Enough Said...

If Looks Could Kill

Men-Tal

The Strength of Guilt and Karma

February 24, 2012, 12 noon Angela sat at her kitchen table with a distressed look on her face. Her eyes looked like she hadn't slept for days; they were red and sort of puffy looking. Life didn't go the way she was taught to believe it would go. She wanted to cry so bad but she had been doing that all night and she was tired of it. I can not believe this actually happened to me. Why couldn't I have been like my mother; the perfect wife. She was loving, took good care of my father, had dinner ready for him when he got off of work. That's the life I wanted. That's the life I thought I had with, Marcello and Marcena. I never would've thought in a million years that my life would turn out fucked up like this. Angela got up and walked outside onto the porch. She looked around at her well manicured street. A few neighbors were outside either shoveling or snow blowing their sidewalks and driveways. It was peaceful; that was the type of life she wanted. When things went sour between her and

Marcello is when things changed for the worst. She started dating other dudes who just weren't right for her. She started getting depressed, even contemplated suicide. She had her daughter to live for. However, she felt like life dealt her an unfair hand. I am a good person. I am a good woman, a good mother; all I wanted was a happy family. Just a simple happy family; I didn't need all of that fancy shit. It's like all of the good people suffer and all of the bad people prosper. What's the use of being good? This shit just aint fair...This shit just aint fair. Unfortunate circumstances in her life eventually got the best of her. And thus gave birth to the hellion, her alter-ego Ms. Nook-Nook. After she stood out there for a few minutes thinking, Marcena came to the door. She opened the screen and leaned out.

"Momma why are you out there in the cold like that? Come in the house; you don't have no coat on." Marcena said.

Angela came out of her daze, turned around, and smiled then said. "You're right sweetie. Just got a lot on my mind right now."

"What's wrong?" Marcena asked as she stepped back so her mom could step back in the house.

Angela slightly smiled at the one person in this world that she loved unconditionally. She grabbed Marcena's hand and led her to the couch and the sat down. Angela kissed Marcena on the forehead, and looked her in her eyes.

"Sweetie, I want the best for you. I need you to do good in life. I need you to be positive and a good loving person, a good wife, a good everything." Angela said.

"I will, momma." Marcena replied.

"Will you promise me you won't be one of these low life females in the street?" Angela asked, as a tear dripped down her face.

Marcena felt disheartened by her mother's tears streaming down her face. She didn't like seeing her mother upset and it made Marcena's eyes water up.

"What's wrong momma?"

Angela shook her head and replied. "I'll be okay. I just need you to keep your promise to me."

"I will." Marcena answered sincerely.

A car pulled up out front; it was Marcena's buddies. They were about to go IHOP.

"Okay, that's Melissa and them. I'll be back later. Okay?" Marcena asked.

"Okay." Angela answered, looking lost.

Marcena just looked at her and asked "Momma, are you gonna be okay? If not, Ima tell them to just leave and I'll stay here with you."

"No, no you go on ahead and have fun. Don't stop enjoying life on the account of me. Ima always love you no matter what." Angela said.

Angela looked at her for a moment still. Melissa blew her horn for Marcena to come on. Marcena looked outside and back at Angela.

"Okay ma, see you in a few." Marcena said and grabbed her coat on and walked out the door.

Angela came to the door just as Marcena was walking out. She had a deep burden troubling her heart. She opened the door and asked "Marcena?"

Marcena turned around and said "Yes mom?"

"I love you."

Marcena smiled and replied, "I love you too."

Angela stood there at the door and watched Marcena get in the car with her friends and pull off. Angela dropped her head and then shut the door. She walked into the den and grabbed her note pad off of the book shelf. She grabbed an ink pen out of an old Planter's peanut can used to pencils, and paperclips etc. She walked to the dinning-room table and sat down. Thoughts of her life were weighing heavy on her heart. She banged on the table very hard out of frustration. Tears fell from her eyes as she tore a sheet of paper from the note book. She laid it on the table and wrote from her heart. Dear Marcena, I love you so much. I can't begin to explain how much you mean to me. You are the sunshine of my day. I remember when you were first born; you were like a little jewel in my arms. You're still my jewel to this day and always will be. However, I do have some things troubling my heart. Things that have been haunting me that I can't escape. I'm sorry if I ever let you down or wasn't a good mother. Please understand that I tried my best. This house is yours and you won't have to struggle in life. Be responsible and take care of it. Take care of yourself. I love you. Angela put her pen down and got up. She walked over to the mantel piece in the living-room and looked at a picture of her and Marcena together. She closed her eyes and kissed it. She sat it back up on the mantle and went and grabbed her coat. She grabbed her purse and headed out the door. She got in her car and pulled off. She turned a few corners and then pulled over at the corner and stopped. She grabbed her check book and pen out of her purse. She wrote out a check to the Mortgage Company paying off the remaining balance of the house. She tore it off and put it in an envelope from out of the glove box. She put the check in it and sealed it up and filled out the front. She grabbed a stamp out of her purse and stuck it on the envelope. She got out of the car, walked over to the mailbox, and dropped it in it. She got back in the car and pulled off. Thoughts ran through her mind as she drove up the road. She hoped that her daughter would forgive her for what she was about to do. She hoped that she wouldn't hate her for what she had done. However, she had to do what she had to do...to escape the skeletons in her mind. She drove up Gratiot, turned down one of the side streets and parked. The time had come... She pulled her pistol out of her purse, looked at it and smirked. Momma always told us not to play with guns; now look atcha. Angela shook her head and placed it under the driver's seat. She got out of the car and locked the door. She turned around and looked at the big building in front of her "1300 Beaubien." She walked across the street, took a deep breath and went inside. She stood in line pitifully shaking her head to herself. When she made it to the front of the line she held her arms out. She handed them her purse and they put it on the conveyor belt and let it ride through the scanner. She held her arms out as they wand her down and let her through. She grabbed her purse, walked over to stand in line. Before today she never would've foresaw turning herself in for a crime she had constructed.

GET AWAY

1:47p.m. the next day Cognac and Devin were loading their luggage in the back of a rental. It was a black 2012 Chrysler 300 looking shiny with the rims gleaming. Devin was coordinating everything so it could fit in the trunk perfectly. Eric senior pulled up, he was coming to pick up little Eric. He was going to keep him while Cognac and Devin were gone. Little Eric was sitting in the living-room with his cloths packed in a duffle bag. He had on his coat and hat. He looked out the window and yelled "MY DAD HERE!!" Eric immediately jumped up and darted for the door. Cognac had to get his attention because he was jetting off to fast. He wasn't thinking about saying goodbye, and didn't grab his bags.

"Hey, hey young road runner, aren't you forgetting something?" Cognac asked.

Eric looked back for a second and said "Oh yeah!" Eric ran back and grabbed his bags and darted to the door! Cognac couldn't believe this lil young fella and said "Ummm

Eric." Eric turned around and said looked around on the floor. He looked at Cognac and said "What I forget?" Cognac replied "Me." Eric dropped his bags and darted over to Cognac. "I'm sorry momma. I love you." Eric said as he gave Cognac a big loving hug. "It's okay son, I love you too. I want you to be good while I'm gone now."

"I will mom, I promise." Eric replied.

"Okay, well we won't keep your daddy waiting to long." Cognac said.

Cognac helped lil Eric with his bags and headed out the door. Eric senior and Devin were standing outside talking.

"Daddy!" Lil Eric said excitedly.

"Hey son. You ready to do this?" Eric Senior asked.

"Yeah." Little Eric replied with a smile.

"Okay, well go ahead and put your stuff in the back seat and let's go."

"Okay." Eric said as he went and put his stuff in the car.

"Hey Rachelle." Eric said as he gave her a respectable hug.

"Hey Eric." Cognac replied with a pleasant smile.

Regina, Reonna and Candace had just pulled up and parked.

"Hey well I aint gone hold y'all up. I know y'all got a long trip ahead of y'all. Y'all let me know y'all made it there safe." Eric said as he headed to his car.

He waved at Regina and them as he got in his ride and pulled off. Regina and everyone came over to get a hug before Cognac and Devin took off. They got out of the car and walked over to them.

"Hey, y'all! We just stopping bye for a second just to give y'all a hug before y'all go." Regina said as she hugged Cognac.

"Aw, thank you boo. I love you so much." Cognac replied.

"I love you too." Regina said.

Regina hugged Devin and said with a smile "Wdup bro? Take care of my cousin on y'all trip."

"Absolutely, that's a given." Devin replied.

Reonna hugged Cognac and said "I brought you a present."

Reonna stepped to the side and Candace walked up and gave Cognac a hug. Cognac was elated to know she was feeling better.

"I'm glad you're feeling a lot better." Cognac said with a smile.

"Thank you. And thank you for always being encouraging and motivating to me. I truly appreciate you." Candace replied.

"Hey, that's what big cousins are for." Cognac replied.

After they kicked it for a moment it was time to go. They finished loading up the car and locked the house up safe and secure. They gave their final hugs and then even got in their cars and pulled off. Cognac smiled because finally she gets to enjoy life and take a break from all of the madness. Devin looked at her and knew that she was happy. He reached over and held her hand. Cognac felt loved. She knew that Devin was a good man and definitely loved her. He was a good role model for son and a good father to his two kids. She had gotten to a point in her life that she was tired of the dating game. She was tired of the emotional rollercoaster ride. She damn sure was tired of all the relationship drama... She smiled as she looked at Devin. She pretty much knew that he was the type of guy she could marry. He possessed all of the qualities she expected from a man and then some. They made a couple of stops getting junk food, and things they wanted for the ride. It was time to hit the highway and head to Miami. Before they got on the freeway they ended up coming upon Elmwood Park Cemetery. Cognac took a deep breath and asked Devin to stop in there, and he did. They cruised around until they found Aunt Val's lot. They looked at each other and then got out of the car. Devin was very concerned about her emotions and how she felt. He gently put his arm around her and walked with her over to the grave. Just as they approached it he let her walk a little further by herself. Just a brief private moment with her and Val is what was needed. Cognac slowly approached it and touched the headstone. She closed her eyes deeply embracing her thoughts and the moment. She kneeled down in front of it. She rubbed her hand across the top of it, brushing the snow off, revealing the name, Mrs. Valerie Davenport.

"You know I miss you so much... You have been my rock and my strength all of my life... It is so hard accepting that you're not here anymore. I miss your delicious meals you'd cook. I miss our insightful conversations... I miss you so much... I'ma try to remember everything you taught me. I promise you I'll make sure Eric is well taken care of... Well, until next time...I love you." Cognac said and got up.

Devin walked up to her and put his arm around her. He carefully walked her back to the car and opened the passenger door for her so she could get in. He went around the other side, got in and they eased off. He asked her if she was okay and she assured him that she was. She put her hand on his and told him thank you for being there for her. After a few moments she was okay. She reached in the back seat and grabbed a brown bag. She pulled out two cups and put them in the cup holders. She pulled out the pint of Hennessey and turned it upside down so he could smack the ass of it. She stroked the neck and head of it a couple of times and then twisted the cap off. She made their drinks, and they tossed on a lil R&B to set the mood just right. And oh yeah...just remember...Aint Nothing Like a lil Cognac...to Getcha Mind Right.

Also By Men-Tal

<u>Salon Talk 4</u>

<u>Why Lie</u>

"Sneak Peek"

MASQUERADE

October 31, 2013, Detroit Michigan, 8:17p.m. Peaches was at home taking a steamy hot shower in her gorgeously decorated bathroom. Scented candles burned in front of her large vanity mirror setting the mood right. Water cascaded down on her sexy honey buttered glazed skin. Any man would've loved the way the soap suds dripped down her figure. She turned the water off, and stepped her sexy feet out on the floor mat. She grabbed her thick, soft bath towel and carefully dried her body off. She grabbed the peach scented lotion off of the shelf and squeezed some in her hand. She rubbed it all over, making sure she didn't miss an inch. She touched her hair up and had it looking sexy as hell. She walked into her bedroom to get dressed. Her cell phone rang and she answered it; it was Cognac calling.

"What up girl?!" Peaches answered, putting the phone on speaker and sitting it on the dresser.

"Damn girl you all hype as hell. You ready?" Cognac asked.

"I'm getting ready right now." Peaches said as she picked up her fishnet leggings off of the bed.

"You must got me on speaker phone because I can't hear you?" Cognac asked.

Peaches grabbed the phone, took it off of speaker and said "My bad, but yeah I'm getting dressed right now."

"Oh okay. What kind of costume you get?" Cognac asked.

"Girl, Ima be a sexy, big booty police officer with some tight ass shorts on." Peaches answered.

"Don't play!" Cognac retorted.

"What? Don't tell me that's what you wearing." Peaches said.

"Well, I guess we gone be two fat booty police officers ready to arrest the first nigga to try to get freaky and feel on our asses." Cognac replied.

"Girl, who don't try to feel on your ass? You got one of them porn star asses." Peaches asked, and laughed.

"Girl, you right along with me. We just gone be the Big Ass Twins tonight. You better be careful, Antonio gone be on your head everywhere you go." Cognac said.

"I know, tell me about it." Peaches said as she went to her kitchen to get her some wine.

"Did y'all ever make it official?"

"Make what official?" Peaches asked as she grabbed her a wine glass from the cabinet.

"You know...y'all...be a couple."

"Oh, oh um...not yet." Peaches answered, reaching in the fridge and pouring her a glass of Merlot.

"Peaches, why you playing and keeping Antonio on hold? Just go ahead and give him a chance."

"I know... I know I've been coming up with excuse after excuse; Ima stop doing that though." Peaches said as she took a nice swallow of her wine.

"Hey look, Ima say this and get out y'all business. Claim that good man before somebody else do, and you be stuck out here with these no good ass dudes."

"You right." Peaches said, taking a deep breath and knowing Cognac was telling her the truth.

"Trust me, it hurts when you find out that somebody got his attention and he aint in to you as much." Cognac preached.

"You right." Peaches said as she poured a little more wine in her glass.

"Okay well look, I'm about to get off of this phone and let your slow self get ready." Cognac said.

"Alright, see you in a minute." Peaches replied and hung up.

Peaches felt good that she was going to tell Antonio she wanted them to be an official couple tonight. She went back into the bedroom all hype and shit. She looked in the mirror and said "I'm locking that nigga ass down tonight! Back up off of my dick bitches because that's my shit! Don't make me have to go HAM and whoop yo ass! What?!" Peaches hit the power button on the stereo in her room and turned on some hype booty shaking music. She danced sexy, admiring her shape in the mirror. She grabbed her fishnets and slid them up her thick ass legs...up over her thick fat bubble ass. She had on a black body suit that read S.W.A.T. on one of the left pocket. She put on her black leather knee high boots. And last but not least she put on her sexy police hat that also read S.W.A.T. She picked up her strawberry lip gloss and traced her perfect kissable lips. She grabbed her little black wind breaker jacket, purse and headed out the door. She immediately walked back in the house and headed to the kitchen. She grabbed a blue plastic cup out of the cabinet and got some more wine out of the fridge. She already had a nice buzz going on and wanted to keep it that way. She left back out the house and hopped in the whip. She turned on the sounds and peeled off. She whipped through the streets for about fifteen minutes and finally reached Antonio's block. She made a right and drove up a few houses, pulled over and parked. She got out and remotely locked the door. She switched beautifully as she walked up on the porch. She knocked hard on the door like she was the police. Antonio was on the phone when Peaches pulled up. He heard the loud knocking and told whoever it was on the phone that he would call them back. He walked to the door, and looked out the peephole. He opened the door and said "Damn, girl knocking like you crazy."

"Shut up and get against that wall!" Peaches said as she stepped in and approached him. Peaches pushed Antonio up against the wall face first like she was the police.

"Oh, you on some ole freaky shit I see." Antonio said as he was being forced up against the wall.

"Spread your fucking legs!" Peaches said as she squatted down and spreaded his legs.

She frisked both of his legs thoroughly. Then she stood up and stepped all of the way up on him. She reached abound him with both of her hands. She started gripping and rubbing all over his hard as dick. She unzipped his pants and reached her hand inside. His warm dick felt good to her hand. She pulled it out and turned his ass around. She pushed him back up against the wall and stared at him seductively. She frowned at him and then bent over and tongue kissed the head of his dick.

"You aint finna get a whole lotta head right now so don't get to thinking that shit! You'll get the rest after the party so be on your best behavior." Peaches said boldly.

Antonio was loving that shit and hated that she stopped.

"So that's how you gone play me?" Antonio asked, standing there with a rock hard dick.

"Yup, now put that juicy black dick back in them pants and let's go!" Peaches said and walked outside.

Antonio just shook his head and stared at her fat ass as she walked out the door. He wanted to fuck the dog shit out of her. It's baby making time later on!!

Also By Men-Tal...

"A Bonus Sneak Peak
At An Urban Street Drama
At its Finest"

1993

DEATH AND DISHONOR

The Year That Changed Our Lives Forever

December 19, 2013, Detroit Michigan, 3:40p.m. A man named Isaac Banner along with his beautiful wife of five years, daughter and son were in line at McDonald's ordering food. The children were very vibrant and chipper. They cheerfully played and picked with each other. The wife was smiling because the kids were all over their father, tugging on his leg. The cashier smiled because it's a beautiful thing to see a happy family. The father looked down at his happy children and asked "Okay pip squeaks what y'all want to get?" They told him what they wanted and he ordered it. They were a good prototypical family. The cashier came back with their food and he paid for it. He grabbed their bags, the mother grabbed the drinks and they left. He opened the door for his wife and kids and they walked out. They headed for their car and then suddenly he stopped. He saw a man standing in the middle of the sidewalk looking at him ominously. The wife and kids stopped as well... She looked at Isaac strange and said "Honey, what's wrong?" He didn't reply he just stood there looking. Again she asked him. "Baby, what's the matter?" And again Isaac didn't respond, he just looked. The strange man's demeanor was subtle, but the look in his eyes was heartless. Isaac felt something tragic was about to happen. He didn't want his family involved in any confrontation. He then looked at his wife with a hopeless bleak stare.

"Take the kids and go to the car." Isaac said to his wife while looking back at the strange man.

"Baby, what are you talking about? Why are you just standing here?" The wife, Karen Matthews asked, wondering what the hell was going on.

"Baby, take the kids to the car now...and take the keys, and food." Isaac said as he handed her the keys.

Karen didn't know exactly what the hell was going on; she just knew that something wasn't right. She took the keys, the food and just looked at Isaac for a second...then she looked at her kids and told them to come on. Carefully they walked on to the car which was just around the corner on the left side of the building. After his family walked away he asked "Where do I know you from?" The strange man just stared at him and then replied "My name is Mr. Hunt." Isaac took a deep breath and sorrowfully dropped his head. He couldn't believe it...after all of these years. He pitifully looked up at the strange man and said "Just don't kill my family...please?" With a cold bleak stare on the strange man's face he pulled out a pistol. He put the barrel right between Isaac's eyes...

...THE YEAR THAT TWISTED HIS LIFE

December 19, 2013, 2:27p.m. Mr. Hunt drove north up Vandyke Rd. It was his birthday and he was on his way to the cemetery. He would go annually to visit and show his respects. He had two bouquets of roses lying on the passenger seat. Ever since the day of drama he never seemed to fully recover from the loss and pain. He finally reached his destination. He looked up at the iron banner just over the top of the entrance. It displayed the name in cold bold black iron letters "Forest Lawn Cemetery." He proceeded inside and around the curvy pathway. All of the tombstones and the above ground sarcophaguses were not very pleasing to the eye. After driving for a couple of minutes he pulled over and parked. He grabbed the roses and got out, shutting the door behind him. It wasn't that much snow on the ground but the ground was hard and cold as hell. He walked across the grass and past numerous tombstones. He thought about that fatal moment that scarred his memory forever. That moment that has brought forth wicked nightmares. Nightmares that have you popping up out of your sleep with buckshot eyes and gasping for breath. He approached the grave lots he was looking for. They lied there buried side by side. He kneeled down and perfectly placed a bouquet at the base of the headstone. He remembered her praying...he remembered hearing the loud rattatat sound of automatic weapons. He remembered the disconsolate screams, and glass flying, shattering on the floor!!... He stood up, and looked at the grave just one space over. He took a deep breath, and stood there for a moment. He then stepped over and kneeled down in front of it. He recalled the fun times; all of the partying, drinking and females. He also remembered some of the troublesome moments; getting shot at and chased by the police. He carefully placed the other bouquet of roses at the base of the headstone. As he got ready to stand up and leave he noticed a number on the head stone that meant so much to him. A number that ran deep in his mind. A number that represented the clique...yeah...1993.

DAY AND NIGHT

July 12, 1993, Detroit Michigan, 5:36p.m. Damn...it wasn't nothing like the good ole days. 2456 Tyler Street and Linwood is where they stayed. Desmond and Carlos were brothers who lived in a home with no father figure in it. They had an ole raggedy ass uncle, Thomas Humphrey, who lived with them. He was anything but a positive role model. Their mother Josephine Humphrey worked eight hours a day at K-Mart, and hadn't made it home yet. She didn't make much and they struggled often. The little bit of valuables they did have in the house they would try to hide them. Uncle Thomas was smoked out again and was known to have sticky fingers. Anyway, Desmond was nineteen and Carlos was twenty. Their personalities were like day and night. Desmond was a pretty good kid and Carlo's had really started becoming a hoodlum. They were in Desmond's room playing Mortal Kombat 2 on the Super Nintendo. They had been playing for a while.

Desmond was whooping Carlos's ass with Shang Tsung. Carlos reached over and tried to push Desmond's joystick.

"Look out bra, stop trying to cheat!" Desmond said.

"Stop crying, nigga and take this ass whooping!" Carlos replied.

"It aint an ass whooping if you gotta try and cheat. That lets me know that you know whose boss." Desmond wittily said.

"Whatever nigga, I'm letting you win so yo ass don't be crying." Carlos replied.

"Nigga, when have you ever known me to be a crying little punk?" Desmond asked.

"Oh it aint like I can't name some, I got a few I can name." Carlos retorted.

"Okay, give me one." Desmond said as he paused the game.

"Okay, okay let me give you one of my all time favorites. Remember that time all I had to do was put a lighter by your head and you would instantly get to crying?"

"Yeah right, I wasn't crying. I would just get mad." Desmond replied.

"Now you gone lie? You would jump scared as hell when I had a lighter in my hand."

"Bra, that's because you set my damn hair on fire when we was little. But what was funny was when momma came in there and started whooping yo ass with that orange industrial extension cord for doing that shit." Desmond replied.

"Yeah that's okay, but it was funny as a muthafucka seeing your hair smoking like you was Ghost Rider running through the house." Carlos said, laughing his ass off.

Desmond all of a sudden got curious. Uncle Thomas shole was quiet as hell. They wondered was he out there trying to steal some shit. He would love to pond some shit so he can go by some blow.

"Aye... Uncle Thomas quiet as hell out there." Desmond said, looking over at Carlos.

"I know. If he's out there trying to steal some shit Ima beat his old ass. Let's creep out there and see." Carlos said.

They quietly got up and crept out of the room. They peeped around the corner into the dinning-room. Uncle Thomas was passed out high as a muthafucka at the table. What was intriguing was the pistol that lied on the table. He must've smoked some serious drugs just to leave a loaded gun on the table. A couple empty cocaine packs lied on the table along with a razor and a straw that was cut in half. Carlos crept over to the table and picked up the gun. He started grinning and ignorantly aiming it around the room. Desmond eased over to convince him to put the gun down.

"Man, put that thing down, you don't even know where that's been. He gone kick yo ass for messing with his shit." Desmond said.

"By who, Uncle T? He aint gone do shit with his high ass. " Carlos said as he playfully aimed it at Desmond.

"Dog, stop playing!" Desmond said.

"See there you go with that crying shit. Look at you crying like a little bitch." Carlos said ignorantly.

"NIGGA, STOP PLAYING DOG BEFORE YOU SHOOT ME WITH THAT THANG!" Desmond said, trying to move out the way of his aim.

"Alright calm down, I'm just playing." Carlos said.

Carlos stood there admiring how the gun looked. Suddenly they heard keys being put in the front door knob! It was momma coming in from work! Carlos hurried and put the gun down on the table and it went off

BOOM!!!!!! Uncle Thomas immediately jumped up scared as fuck like the end of the world was here! He had a stupid ass look on his face and glossy wide eyes from smoking that dope. The bullet barely grazed Desmond's shirt. If he would've never tried to move he would've been shot and probably killed. Josephine hurried up and rushed in the house! Her heart raced like hell as she wondering what was going on. She just hoped her two babies and her brother were okay.

"What the hell is going on in here?!" Josephine asked as she walked into the dinning-room.

Desmond looked at his shirt in disbelief, and then looked at Carlos. Carlos stood there momentarily flabbergasted thinking he had shot his brother. Josephine looked at them incredulity as Carlos and Desmond stood there. She looked at the dumbfounded, high look on Uncle Thomas's face. She looked at the gun on the table and saw where it was aimed. Then she looked over at Carlos who looked like he had just fucked up. Then she looked over at Desmond as he shamefully looked at her. He was holding the edge of his shirt where the bullet went clean through. She quickly walked over to him and lifted his shirt to see if he was hit. She saw that he was okay and looked back at Carlos.

"What the hell you doing with a gun in my house? Don't you know that thang can kill somebody?" Josephine asked.

"I...I didn't think it was gone go off." Carlos replied.

"Where the hell you get a gun from anyway?!" Josephine asked.

"It's not mine." Carlos said with a face full of fear.

Josephine looked over at Desmond and asked "Desmond?..."

"It's not mines, I swear!" Desmond answered.

Thomas stood his high ass up; unable to stand without wavering and said "It's my damn gun! But I aint tell they asses to touch it, either!"

Josephine wanted to slap the shit out of him with that gun! She was wroth!

"I let you stay yo sorry ass in my house and this is how you repay me?! Endangering my sons, and snorting dope at my table! Thomas...really...you bring a gun in my house and irresponsibly leave it out and my son almost gets killed?" Josephine uttered.

Thomas just stood there wavering back and forth, high as a kite. White residue around his nostrils and bucked eyes.

"Thomas, take this damn gun and get the hell out of my house and don't come back!!!" Josephine yelled with a face full of rage!

Thomas stood there for a second. He looked over at the boys. Wobbling back and forth he grabbed the gun off the table and managed to put it in his waistline. He gave them a nasty hazy look and managed to walk out the door.

A Lil Cognac Ta Get Ya Mind Right Alright, for the time being I'm the Topic of Discussion. Who am I you ask? I'm Rachelle, but my friends call me Cognac or Coney for short because when-ever we're having a discussion or I have an opinion about something I give it to you straight with no ice, and no cola. So if you can't handle the truth then I suggest that you keep your mouth shut and your thoughts to yourself. However, I'm sort of messed up in the head right now because I'm sitting here in my GORGEOUS kitchen staring at the glass from my BEAUTIFUL kitchen table shattered all over the floor and a trail of blood leading out the front door. Now I'm sure you would like to know what the hell is going on here, but look...I need yall to give me a moment to clean this mess up, take me a good hot bath, and get dressed. Its ladies night over at Lacey's Bar and Grill so just meet me over there and I'll explain to you what just happened... Blood is too hard to get off the floor if you leave it on there for too long...Damn I need a drink. Sincerely Cognac

<u>Salon Talk 2 – 187 Degrees of Danger</u>

Perhaps I'm paying for the sins of my past life... With every step I take towards peace and prosperity the wicked always seem to show itself. Have I not given enough...to overshadow anything I've taken? *HAVE I NOT PRAYED AND ASKED FOR FORGIVNESS ENOUGH?!!!* I'm trying to right my wrongs!... I remember that night...vaguely...I remember him sitting there... I remember the bright lights... I remember that loud engine roaring!! *I REMEMBER THE TRAUMATIZING CRACKING SOUND OF GUNFIRE!!..* I remember the blood... I remember the blood spilling...My heart beating...slowly...I feel nothing...

SPIT

As if the pain was not enough ...witnessing the murder of his childhood peers and having his best friend, Diangelo take his last breath in his arms...As if the deception, controversy, relationship issues, nightlife and violence is not enough to make a good man loose his sanity and religion... sometimes the micro-phone and spotlight is a man's sanctuary and redemption ...Life...is like a loaded gun pointed at your head leaving you with two options live or die and one question...What would you do?

Silent Screams

Silent Screams is a collection of thought provoking poems that elaborate on the many aspects of our lives ranging from love, relationships, intimacy, and much more.

Salon Talk: A Topic of Discussion, SPIT and Silent Screams are available for purchase on your major online book sites

Contact Information Page

Men-Tal
Novelist/ Poet/ Art Illustrator
CEO of Essential Expressions
Wordsmith for personalized cards
For Birthdays, Holidays Greetings, Weddings
Baby Showers, Just because, Condolence etc.
Facebook info: SalonTalk MenTal
Facebook book club: Salon Talk Book club
Twitter info: @SalonTalkTheNovel
Email: WritingExtraordinaire@yahoo.com

Gentle Touch Phlebotomy Education, LLC
Chantelle R. White CEO/ Director/ Instructor
23300 Greenfield RD Suite 212
Oak Park MI, 48237
Gentletouch.org
"Where drawing blood is more than a skill it's an art"
"We're changing lives one blood draw at a time"

AIM- All In Mind Designs
Maurice Ingram
Graphics Designer/ Art Illustrator

Hanufel8@yahoo.com

TVJ PHOTOGRAPHY
Jay Jones
Published Photographer
(313)618-6483
Jayrizee@gmail.com

Grand Diva's Hair and Nail Salon
Cocoa
Hair Stylist
(313)350-4024
Grand.diva@comcast.net

Qrispstyle
Quichard Cunningham
Handmade/custom jewelry and accessory
design
Also book Editor
(248)905-1151
Qrispstyle@gmail.com